A City of Dreams

DEDICATION

*To Pat and Julie and
their cats—*

Martha and The Rat

A CITY OF DREAMS

SIGMUND BROUWER

VICTOR BOOKS

A DIVISION OF SCRIPTURE PRESS PUBLICATIONS INC.
USA CANADA ENGLAND

THE WINDS OF LIGHT SERIES
Wings of an Angel
Barbarians from the Isle
Legend of Burning Water

The Forsaken Crusade
A City of Dreams
Merlin's Destiny

Cover design by Mardelle Ayres
Cover illustration by Jeff Haynie
Photo by Dwight Arthur

Library of Congress Cataloging-in-Publication Data

Brouwer, Sigmund, 1959–
   A city of dreams / by Sigmund Brouwer.
      p.   cm. — (The Winds of light ; 5)
   Summary: In the early fourteenth century the boy warrior Thomas, still trying to save the earldom of Magnus from the false sorcerer Druids who have overrun it, wanders the Holy Land in search of knights who survived the end of the Last Crusade.
   ISBN 1-56476-048-0
   [1. Knights and knighthood—Fiction. 2. Civilization, Medieval—Fiction. 3. Palestine—Fiction. 4. Druids and druidism—Fiction. 5. Christian life—Fiction.] I. Title. II. Series: Brouwer, Sigmund, 1959- Winds of light series ; #5.
PZ7.B79984Ci   1993
[Fic]—dc20
                                                    92-41070
                                                       CIP
                                                        AC

1   2   3   4   5   6   7   8   9   10   Printing/Year   97   96   95   94   93

VICTOR BOOKS
A division of SP Publications, Inc.
Wheaton, Illinois 60187

AUTHOR'S NOTE

The "Winds of Light" series follows the adventures of the boy warrior, Thomas of Magnus, whose tale begins in England in the early 1300s.

Thomas' entire story spans six volumes, though each book tells a complete tale on its own. *Wings of an Angel*, the first book in the series, describes how the orphan Thomas—then 14 and old enough to be considered a man—conquered the kingdom of Magnus and released its village from murderous oppression. He is aided by the mysterious young woman, Katherine, whose adventures also unfold throughout the series. We also meet Sir William, a wandering knight; Tiny John, a young pickpocket; self-serving Waleran; and Isabelle, a mute slave girl.

The second volume of the story of Magnus *(Barbarians from the Isle)* tells how Thomas battled the powerful northern Scots. He then faced a far greater trial, one imposed by Druid false sorcerers who demanded Thomas join their secret group or lose his lordship and his castle. We meet the powerful Earl of York and learn more of Katherine and her companion, an old man with special knowledge and power.

A victory against the Druids enabled Thomas to keep Magnus, but as the third volume *(Legend of Burning Water)* reveals, his victory was only temporary. Posing as false priests, the Druids regained Magnus. Thomas was forced to flee and take desperate action, guided by strangers he dared not trust, strangers who knew all the truth behind Magnus. Helping Thomas battle the Priests of the Holy Grail were Robert of Uleran, Thomas' faithful sheriff and Gervase, a priest who truly loves God.

In the fourth portion of the tale, *The Forsaken Crusade*, Thomas held ransom what he believed was his single last chance to regain Magnus. Yet he failed, lost his hostage Isabelle, and escaped England across dangerous seas to the Holy Land, accompanied by a puppy who had saved his life. In the Holy Land he again encountered the mysterious young woman, Katherine, whose path had crossed his own so often.

A City of Dreams begins in St. Jean d'Acre, where Thomas and Katherine have been abruptly reunited with the wandering knight, Sir William.

In that ancient town, 22 years had passed since the last banner of any German, English, and French crusader knights had flown above its stone walls, casting shadows upon the Mediterranean waters below. The town then had been a riot of colors. Merchants from 11 European countries had competed for sales from their great *fonduks*—large, open-squared warehouses—all supplied from ships arriving from the sea on one side and from camel caravans led by Arab traders arriving by the Damascus road on the other.

Yet after nearly 200 years as the main port to the Holy Land, St. Jean d'Acre, the last of the crusader strongholds in the Holy Land, had finally fallen to Muslims. Now the town was a mere shell of the trading center it had been. To be sure, merchants still haggled, for occasional ships still arrived. But the walls of the city and the high turrets of its remaining buildings were war-ravaged and doomed to crumble to dust with age.

Few now were those with fair skin and blue eyes, the sure signs of northern European heritage. And none were those who dared display the colors of any knighthood among the Muslims—who so thoroughly dominated the land that Jesus Christ Himself had walked during His brief and significant life on earth 1,300 years earlier.

Though St. Jean d'Acre existed in fact, those interested in ancient times should know that Magnus itself cannot be found in any history book. Nor can Thomas be found, nor others of his friends and foes. Yet many of the more famous people and events found throughout this story shaped the times of that medieval world, as historians may easily confirm.

THOMAS
St. Jean d'Acre: The Past Unfolds
LATE SUMMER A. D. 1313

Deep within the inner town of St. Jean d'Acre—crowded with square flat houses darkened by early evening—a knight jammed an iron bar across the inside of his door, then turned to the two reasons for the hasty barricade.

"These are not the circumstances I envisioned for a joyful reunion," Sir William told his two visitors. "Yet when one prays for a miracle, one does not ask the Lord to make it a *convenient* miracle."

The closest visitor smiled—unseen—as she unfurled the veil which covered her face.

The other visitor, Thomas of Magnus, merely gazed about the room with undisguised wonder and awe. "I have been here before," he said, "many times in strange and troubled dreams."

"You have reason for this familiarity. You spent a part of your childhood in this house," Sir William said softly. "Would that I had time now to explain."

Thomas saw the knight's face did not reflect his urgency,

despite the recent echoes of that iron bar slammed quickly down. His rugged and handsome face—that of a trained fighter—had changed little since the knight departed from Thomas a year and two continents before. Sir William was still darkly tanned, his hair cropped short now, with a trace of gray at the edges. His blue eyes were still as deep as they were careful to hide thoughts. And, as always, that ragged scar ran down his right cheek.

Shaking away his trance, Thomas half laughed. "Explain? I'm in this town less than half a day after stepping off ship—" furrows across his forehead deepened as he shot a dark glance at the other visitor "—and out of the chains which held me there because of Katherine. A half day, yet already I've been forced to flee assassins, only to have you appear as rescuer. You, a person I never expected see again. Then, in one breath outside those doors, you tell me my father is alive and waits for me, and in another breath inside this house you tell me that I spent part of my childhood here, in a land thousands of miles away from England."

Thomas paused. "Only a *sane* man would demand explanation of all these mysteries." He then shrugged and smiled to rob his sarcasm of insult. "However, *no* man could be *sane* under these circumstances. So do not trouble yourself with tiresome explanations. Even if we had the time."

The third person in the room shook her hair loose as the veil finally fell away. The light of the lamps burnished her blond hair, so that it appeared almost bronze. Her suddenly revealed beauty drew a gasp from Sir William.

"Katherine," he marveled. "I remember you a winsome child, but this . . . this. . . . " He stopped and sighed as if love struck. "Were I as young as Thomas, I would throw myself at your feet and pledge the treasure of all the earth."

His stunned reaction showed how little the knight cared

for finery. Katherine wore a long cape of purple silk, held in place at the neck by an oval clasp of silver which showed an engraved sword. Her neck and wrists glittered with exquisite jewelry. Yet he had seen all of that—an impressive sight anywhere, let alone the depths of this ancient port town—and had not glanced twice.

But now, he noted Katherine's inner joy which added beauty to a face revealing delicate curves and a hint of mystery. Again, William sighed theatrically.

Katherine laughed. "Death pursues us, but you men think only of desire." She laughed again. "And to pledge the earth's treasure is farthest from the mind of your friend Thomas. He much prefers threats, such as casting me from ships at sea."

The knight widened his eyes in mock horror, but his reply was interrupted by shouts from outside. Moments later, a crash sounded as a heavy shoulder pounded the wooden door.

Then, two more crashes. The iron bar held secure.

Shouts again.

"By the sounds, perhaps a dozen men," the knight said.

Another crash shook the door in its frame.

"Your crossbow will be useless at short quarters," Thomas said, nodding at the weapon the knight had laid upon a nearby table. "Have we a place to our advantage in a sword fight?"

The knight shook his head. "Against infidel assassins, no place gives advantage."

"I will not die quietly," Thomas vowed.

"Who speaks of death?" the knight countered.

Sir William yanked an unlit lamp from a nearby shelf. He pulled the wick loose from the base and emptied the oil in a semi-circle on the room's wooden furnishings. He then grabbed one of the three burning lamps and shattered it on the ground.

Flames licked at the spilled oil, then burst into a small wall of fire.

The knight nodded grimly as black smoke began to fill the room. "Let them fight this instead."

2

Had Thomas been able to see his own reaction to the unexpected fire, he would have been slightly amused, not at his lack of panic, but at how well his childhood training served him during times of battle. For even as the flames around them began to roar, assumptions and conclusions raced through his mind.

The knight has no intention of suicide. Therefore, he must have an escape planned.

The knight wasted no time gathering valuables before setting this fire. Therefore, he must have placed his valuables elsewhere.

Yet the meaning of those two conclusions is staggering. The knight has been ready to flee this house in an instant. He has anticipated this very moment!

How? Why?

The answers, Thomas vowed, would come later. Now—as shouting outside rose in response to the smoke which poured through the window openings carved in the limestone walls—was the time to follow the knight.

Sir William silently gestured for Katherine and Thomas to follow. He led them through a narrow archway into another chamber of the house.

This chamber leads to two others, thought Thomas. *I know this without doubt. There will be arched windows in one, a statue of Mother Mary in the other. And, during the morning, sunlight will stream across the statue as it did so many times when I sat on the floor and reached for lazy flies and listened to . . . .*

Thomas felt his heart skip a beat. Even in the haste of escape, the memories returned. This was no dream. No visit during sleep so real that he woke with unexplained tears nearly dry across his face.

I sat in this very house! My childhood nurse spent time with me in these very rooms!

Sir William led them farther, to the room which indeed contained the statue of Mother Mary. He then stooped suddenly and began to pry at the edge of one of the flat stones on the floor. Behind them was the heat of the rapidly growing fire as it spread into another chamber.

No words were yet spoken.

The stone moved aside. Below it, a large iron ring was recessed into wood.

Sir William flipped the ring upward. There was enough room in the circle of the ring for him to use both hands.

He grunted, a sound barely heard above the fire. He grunted again as he pulled, and an entire section of the floor lifted.

"Take a lamp," he instructed Thomas. "Descend and wait."

Thomas moved quickly across the room, grabbed the lamp base and held it steady and level as he rejoined Sir William and Katherine. He looked into the darkness of the hole in the floor.

"Go quickly," the knight said. "There are steps. Katherine

and I will follow."

Briefly, Thomas wondered if this was a trap. He did not yet trust Katherine fully. And by association, neither should he fully trust the knight.

He considered whether to hand the lamp to Katherine, to send her down first instead.

"Quickly," the knight urged. "I hear them breaking through the door!"

Thomas dropped down. Almost immediately, Katherine followed. With light in hand, it was not difficult now to see the downward path of the crooked steps.

Darkness closed over them as the trapdoor above lowered. The wick's flame flickered at the sudden rush of air, but Thomas protected it quickly with his upper body and the flame stayed alive.

He felt a hand on his shoulders. A soft touch.

"Thomas," Katherine's voice whispered.

His eyes adjusted to the dimness, and he held the lamp high as he descended.

"Thomas," Katherine repeated.

He shook his concentration away from the tunnel which grew in his vision ahead and below.

"Yes," he whispered back. *Where did the tunnel lead?*

"Sir William," Katherine said. "He is not with us."

3

Thomas set the lamp down, placed one hand on the hilt of his sword, and turned to move back past Katherine, one step above him.

"No," she pleaded. "We cannot return."

"And let him die alone?" Thomas asked.

Katherine placed her hands on his shoulders as he attempted to push up the steps. "Or die together? Sir William chose to remain behind. Our deaths up there will only make his sacrifice useless."

Thomas was that one step lower, and it brought his face directly to the level of hers. For an insane moment, Thomas forgot the fire, the mysteries, and the fight above. Katherine's scent filled him as surely as the softness of her hair against his face reminded him of the touch of her arms on his shoulders.

Her eyes widened in the faltering light of the lamp, as if she too had suddenly become aware that time and circumstances had fallen away.

Thomas felt her hands behind his neck begin to clasp as the pressure of her downward push on his shoulders eased and instead became the beginning of an embrace. He swayed slightly and closed his eyes. In that insane moment, he wanted to remove his hand from his sword and pull her even closer.

Insanity! Katherine may be one of the Druids! In spite of all they had endured together, Thomas was filled with suspicion.

He opened his eyes. Her eyes were closed in trust. *Such beauty.* It brought him an ache of joy to think of an eternity of her love.

Insanity! A friend above gives his life that we may flee!

She sensed his hesitation. Opened her eyes. Broke the spell.

"M'lady," Thomas began to apologize.

"Thomas," she said in the same moment.

They both stopped in midsentence.

Awkwardly, Thomas stepped back and down from her.

"Surely this tunnel leads to escape," he said quickly. Anything to break away from the spell of her presence. "Sir William would not have planned it otherwise. And the fire above will lead the town to panic. We must hurry to keep our advantage."

"And then?"

Thomas did not reply. He had no answer, and for that reason wanted only to concentrate on ducking through the low tunnel as he guarded the wick of his lamp from the water which dripped from the cool stone.

When they stopped to rest ten minutes later, Thomas was ready with his questions.

"Tell me," he said, determined to ignore the effect of her nearness, "of matters of my childhood."

"How is it I should know?" she asked, almost aloof, as if

she too sought to distance herself from tender feelings.

"You . . . you are a Merlin." Thomas hoped she would not hear any doubt in his voice, though it filled his heart. "And Sir William also opposes the Druids. He too is a Merlin. Surely you and he have secrets in common."

"We are indeed Merlins," Katherine said. "Yet the Druids' conquest of Magnus forced many surviving Merlins into isolation. Sir William roamed the world, while I remained in disguise among the Druids of Magnus. How much can I know of his part in our battle against those evil ones?"

Even now she holds back truth, Thomas thought with a trace of bitterness. *And I long to trust her and hold her and. . . .* He forced himself to concentrate on his questions.

"When those assassins pursued us from the marketplace," he said, "you led us not to the inn, where we left our belongings but directly to the house where Sir William waited. Is that not proof of shared knowledge?"

His words echoed softly in the stone tunnel and many heartbeats passed before she replied.

"Yes, indeed," she finally began. "When Magnus fell to the Druids, Sir William, your parents, and a handful of others barely escaped with their lives. England was no longer safe. So they fled here, to the Holy Land, hoping . . . hoping to find help in fighting the Druids from the valiant Crusaders."

Had her hesitation been a shiver of cold? Or a lie? Thomas chose to remain silent, to wait for more.

"You and I," Katherine said, "were raised here, in the house that so troubled your dreams. Your father dared not return to England. Druid spies were everywhere, and to be recognized in England would give them too much warning that not *all* the Merlins of Magnus had died. When the time was right, you and I were smuggled back to England. While I served in disguise as a spy in Magnus, you were trained in that obscure abbey by Sarah, one of the most dedicated Merlins of her generation. Our hope was that you might remain unknown to the Druids—and close enough to reconquer Magnus with the knowledge given to you. It was a small hope, and with Sarah's death, even smaller."

Thomas closed his eyes at the name of his childhood nurse. *Sarah had tutored him relentlessly in games of mathematics and logic. She had corrected him with endless patience as he painfully learned to read and write in the world's major languages. And in all those hours and days and years of instruction, she had favored him with a love deeper than any. . . .* "It cannot be," Thomas whispered.

"Thomas?" Katherine had caught the pain in his voice.

He faltered as he spoke. "I arrived at the abbey as a child. I can remember—dimly—those first days there. You tell me that the *earliest* years of my life were spent here—in St. Jean d'Acre. That I understand and believe, for my understanding of this land's foreign tongue is proof enough."

He paused as another memory struck him: the memory of the first moment he saw Katherine's face in the moonlight— nearly a year ago. Nothing in his life had prepared him for that moment. He had learned—from betrayal by the beautiful, dark-haired Isabelle—not to trust appearance to reveal a person's heart. Yet then, in the shadows of the moonlight, he felt as if he had been long pledged to the woman with the mysterious smile in front of him. Katherine. Known since childhood.

And later, on the castle's ramparts when he had first stolen from her a kiss, the same certainty filled him. What a bond they must have forged as small children, laughing and playing here in St. Jean d'Acre, unaware of the roles they must later play in a battle against the very Druids who had slain so many of their parents' friends.

His bond with Katherine — and the foreign language of the marketplace which seemed so natural — was solid proof of the childhood Thomas could not remember.

But was it solid proof that she was indeed a Merlin? Could she be trusted as he tried to make sense of all that had been hidden? Thomas pushed those thoughts aside, and pursued the one thought which had first caused his voice to falter.

"As a boy, I believed I was an orphan, that Sarah was raising me at the abbey on the strength of money left to the church by my father, who had been a wealthy mason. You tell me instead, that I was raised in secret as a Merlin to be part of a centuries-old battle against the unseen Druids. You say *both* my parents were part of that battle."

Thomas shook his head. "I can scarcely take all of this in." His voice grew shakier. "May parents were *alive* then, not fallen to the plague as I had been told. Sir William says my father is here in the Holy Land. Could it be that Sarah, the nurse who guided and loved me as truly as a mother . . . could it be she *was* my mother?"

Katherine's silence in the tunnel's darkness was answer enough.

Thomas did not wipe away his tears of renewed grief. To have lost a mother twice . . . .

Katherine closed her eyes and shared quietly in his pain.

Neither had a chance to compose more conversation. For above the steady dripping of water against stone, came the far-away echo of approaching footsteps.

4

Immediately, Katherine reached between them to pinch the wick of the lamp. Thomas grasped her wrist and held it steady.

"This light will betray our presence," she protested.

Thomas thought of another time, beneath the castle of Magnus, when blind stumbling through secret passageways had nearly cost him his life. He did not release her wrist.

"How shall we light the lamp again?" he asked. "For without light, we might never leave this tunnel."

He then smiled. "And did not your training as a Merlin teach you the words of a wise general now long dead?" He paused. "All warfare is deception."

Her answer was a silent stare. Almost as if to deny their moment of unexpected closeness earlier, she seemed too proud to smile in return, too proud to attempt to free her wrist from his grip, and too proud to admit her unfamiliarity with the quote.

The footsteps grew louder.

"Deception is what we will practice now," said Thomas. He released Katherine's wrist, lifted the lamp, and carried it forty steps back in the direction from which they had started.

He set the lamp down and rejoined Katherine in the darkness.

"Now," he said, "when our visitor approaches, he will expect us there, ahead at the light, instead of here in the shadows."

First Katherine and Thomas saw an approaching glow, then the light of the visitor's lamp, still too far away to let them identify the holder of that lamp. The visitor's footsteps slowed, however, and stopped almost as soon as the light had appeared.

This stranger sees our own light ahead, Thomas thought, *and hesitates.*

In the next moment, that faraway light disappeared.

The visitor chooses to approach now in darkness. From caution born of fear, or caution born of evil intent?

No longer could Thomas or Katherine hear footsteps.

This visitor must pass close enough to touch us. But how soon?

Thomas nearly yelped at a sudden touch against his hand. His heart slowed quickly, though, as soon as he realized Katherine had slipped her fingers among his.

They waited, side by side.

Then Thomas felt, rather than heard, the nearness of a stranger, almost as if the only hint of another person was air pushed ahead in the stillness of the tunnel.

Does this stranger walk with dagger or sword poised? Will I leap ahead into a sudden death?

Thomas did not answer his own silent question, for he had

been taught that hesitation was the greatest enemy in the
moment of action in any battle. He had also been taught the
advantage of the terror of noise.

Thomas bellowed a rage that filled the tunnel as he
charged into the stranger. His shoulder rammed a solid bulk.
Hands were upon him instantly and Thomas punched back.
Twice he hit only air, but three times his knuckles jarred
against bone. Thomas continued to roar in anger as he
lashed out again and again at the unseen stranger.

They tumbled and rolled. The stranger was heavier, but
Thomas was faster and more desperate.

Their fight soon became silent, for Thomas had no energy
to continue the roar of attack. Heavy breathing filled his face.
Hands once managed to wrap around his neck, but Thomas
lashed out with his knee to strike hard flesh, and the hands
released with a grunt of pain, only to seek him again from
the darkness.

Thomas felt a face and tried to push away with the heel of
his palm.

Another grunt, then a glancing blow against his cheek-
bone, and he fell back with flashes of light filling his eyes.

Then dimly, he heard it.

"Stop," Katherine was yelling. "Both of you stop!" And
Thomas realized the light in his eyes was now the light of
the lamp that Katherine had brought closer.

"Stop!" Katherine repeated from where she stood above
them both.

Thomas felt his opponent relax and roll away from him, so
he too relaxed and struggled to his feet.

The voice which greeted him was all too familiar.

"Should demons ever assume earthly form," Sir William
said, attempting a chuckle that became a cough of pain, "that
form would closely resemble Thomas of Magnus."

Thomas groaned and began to feel his body for broken bones. "And should humans ever assume the forms of ghosts," he said as he probed his mouth for shattered teeth, "they would do well to imitate Sir William. For considerate humans would announce their presence to friends."

Sir William staggered slightly as he tried to straighten. "I saw the lamp, but no one near. I could only assume the worst and wonder how best to approach the enemies which had captured you."

Katherine moved forward and examined Sir William's face for cuts. "We thought you dead," she said softly.

"My own face fares poorly," Thomas hinted.

She ignored him.

"What happened?" Katherine asked Sir William. "In the house? In the fire?"

"I'll tend to my own bruises," Thomas announced, but still Katherine ignored him.

Sir William wordlessly took the lamp from Katherine's hand, returned to his own lamp, and relit it. In the circle of renewed light, he sat and leaned against the tunnel wall with a moan.

"Join me," he said. "In the little time before the caravan leaves, I have much to explain, and here in the tunnel is much safer than above."

Katherine stepped forward and Thomas limped closer. It hurt him to sit. But it also hurt to stand.

"The events in the house?" Sir William began. "I wanted to lead the assassins away from the house and the tunnel. But I also feared if I told you I planned to fight and flee by another door, neither of you would agree to accept the safety of this tunnel. So I fought briefly, escaped the house, led the assassins on a merry chase, then entered this tunnel by a hidden exit we shall reach soon."

He turned to Thomas. "As you might guess, this escape had been ready for years. The Merlins have owned the house for generations—almost since the beginning of the Crusades—and have often used this tunnel for the arrival and departure of visitors who should not be seen in town."

"But why here in St. Jean d'Acre?" Thomas asked. It was difficult not to continue probing his ribs for bruises, but he did not want to give Sir William the satisfaction. "We are across the world from Magnus. What significance has this town to the Merlins? Or to the Druids?"

Sir William nodded. "The town itself only has significance because it is the traditional entry for those traveling to the Holy Land by ship."

He let that statement hang in the silence until Thomas spoke.

"You say then that it is the Holy Land which draws *both* Merlins and Druids?"

Sir William nodded. "And Druid spies, as do ours, watch the ships as passengers enter the town. I believe the symbol on Katherine's clasp—so prominent on her cloak—led them to discover you quickly."

Yes, Thomas thought. *A begger in the market* had *inquired of the clasp's value. And Katherine firmly said it was a family heirloom. The distinct sword engraved in the clasp, then, what is its meaning? A secret sign of the Merlins perhaps?*

Thomas was given no time to ponder, for the knight continued to speak.

"Both sides seek a great secret lost here in the Holy Land centuries ago," Sir William said. "The search has stretched over generations. The side which first discovers that secret will have the power to destroy the other."

5

What strangeness is this? Thomas wondered. *I am here beneath the streets of a town in the land where Christ once walked, with sudden knowledge of my lost childhood, in quiet conversation with a knight who once saved my life and helped me win a kingdom, and—if Katherine's story during our sea voyage is to be believed—I have been destined to continue a centuries-old battle against a secret circle of evil.*

Thomas laughed softly.

Sir William glanced at him, puzzlement clear even in the flickering light of the lamps.

"You find humor in this?"

Thomas stood and spoke as he ran his fingers along the rough stone of the tunnel walls.

"It is only because I feel the coldness of this stone that I can believe this is not a dream of madness," Thomas said. "Laughter? How else might one face the storms of life?"

"Well spoken," Sir William said. "And this is indeed a storm. I have not yet heard what troubles have led you here to the Holy Land. Katherine, I am sure, will tell me the sad news later, during the long hours of travel that face us."

Thomas raised an eyebrow. "Katherine? Not I?" Instinctively, he dropped his hand to his sword. "Do you imply that I will not be there?"

Sir William groaned and raised a hand as if fending off attack. "Must you be so untrusting? Did I not help you to secure Magnus from the Druids?"

"Trust is the one thing I wish I could possess," Thomas said softly. "While much has been *explained*, too little real knowledge has yet been given me."

He stared directly at Sir William and Katherine, considering the reasons for his mistrust. "That day at the gallows long ago," Thomas challenged. "Why was the old man there? The same old man who so myseriously appeared later with Katherine as they followed me throughout England? And you too, Sir William. Why were you there at the gallows with the old man? I cannot believe in coincidence."

The knight answered, "We were there because of the songs Sarah had taught you as a child. Think back, Thomas. Had she not always told you about a *knight* who would appear from the land of the sun?"

Thomas nodded. He remembered that. He remembered Sarah's instructions. He remembered too the chant she had taught him, the chant he had heard later from the people of Magnus, that the one to reconquer Magnus would arrive as if *delivered on the wings of an angel*. Thomas remembered how Sarah had again and again told him to wait for the *one knight* he would need to free Magnus.

And he remembered her love. *Sarah had been his mother, and not once had they been able to share that knowledge.* Thomas spun away from Sir William and Katherine and bowed his head as spasms of grief shook him.

Katherine rose quickly and placed a comforting arm around Thomas.

"No," he said, not harshly, as he straightened. "This is not a time for grief. This is a time for answers."

Katherine stepped back, then slowly sat and rejoined the knight in the lamplight.

Thomas drew a deep breath. *Later, alone, he would spend time among memories and say farewell properly to the woman who had given so much of her life to him.*

Thomas exhaled. His voice remained steady as he spoke again. "You *expected* me then, to appear at the gallows that day?"

"Yes," Sir William said. "How else might we get you to come forth without exposing ourselves to unseen and unknown Druids?"

"Yet had I not appeared," Thomas countered, "you would have swung from the rope."

Sir William shook his head in gentle disagreement. "The old man was there. Had you not appeared, he would have saved my life and we would have begun our search for you."

"Saved your life?" Thomas asked.

Sir William now nodded. "After all, he had arranged the time of execution to match that of the darkness of the sun."

Thomas gaped. "The old man had such worldly power?"

Katherine's unnatural stillness suddenly drew his attention, and Thomas stopped, mouth still open before uttering his next words.

Sir William too turned his attention to Katherine.

"The old man is dead," Katherine said with the quietness of extreme pain.

"Dead?" The word was uttered in disbelief. But you did not speak of—"

"Dead," Katherine repeated. "Magnus is in the hands of

the Druids, they rapidly expand their power among the people of North England, and the old man is dead."

The knight stood quickly. Urgency now filled his voice.

"Thomas, our continued survival is of utmost importance. All the more reason, then, that we separate now and travel apart. The assassins will be searching for three. And you, or Katherine and I must reach our destination."

Sir William turned to Katherine. "He shall go by caravan. You and I travel on foot. Tell me all during our journey. I must not delay in giving instructions to Thomas."

"Katherine," Thomas said. "That puppy we left with our belongings at the inn. We cannot leave it to die there."

"It shall be taken care of," Sir William said quickly, wanting the discussion to end.

Then Sir William took his lamp and began to lead them forward. Some thirty steps later—where he had first darkened his own lamp to approach with such caution—Sir William stooped to retrieve a package.

He gave it to Thomas.

"This must remain sealed. Guard it with every fiber of your body and soul," Sir William said. "Too much of our battle against the Druids depends on its safe arrival—with you—in Jerusalem. After we visit Nazareth."

"Nazareth," Thomas repeated.

"Yes. For your father awaits you there."

6

Thomas woke to great shrieking groans. Startled and confused, he sat straight up, unconscious of the blanket dropping away from his upper body.

The light around him was dim and diffused to a hazy pale, and it took great effort for him to distinguish from that light the tent walls which surrounded him.

The great shrieking groans grew louder.

Then he heard giggles behind him.

He clutched the blanket and swung around to see two veiled servant girls, one carrying a pitcher, the other a basin. Their giggles continued.

Thomas mustered as much dignity as possible.

"The sound of madness outside?" He stumbled through those words in their Arabic language, so strange yet so familiar. "Is it not early in the day for torture and executions?"

More giggles.

Before Thomas could inquire further, the tent flaps swirled open and a large figure entered, dark against the sunlight which streamed in behind his back.

"Be gone!" the figure roared. "Leave this man in peace!"

The girls merely giggled again, and only when the large man advanced with a raised, threatening hand did they hitch their skirts and run past him, still giggling.

It was the Arab, Muzzamar. Thomas had only seen him briefly the night before, and then only in the light of a small torch as he and Sir William bartered with great animation.

Though Muzzamar was obviously fat, even with the layers of fine and colorful cloth draped around him, this man moved with a softness that suggested athletic grace. His eyes, almost lost within that broad face, were sharp. The gray goatee was well trimmed. The deep lines around his mouth showed years of laughter, yet no man reached his age and position without the ability to dispatch the most vicious enemy, and Thomas warned himself to be on guard.

Muzzamar groaned as he lowered himself to sit on a stool near Thomas. "This generation has little respect for their elders. In my youth, I would have been whipped for hesitation to obey any command."

The large man continued a steady stream of complaints, but used the noise of his own words as a screen while his sharp eyes studied Thomas. During the previous night, their meeting had been hurried, and most of the attention had been on the knight who carried the purse of gold and negotiated a price of safe passage for this young stranger.

The large man saw quiet strength in Thomas, a calmness that seemed more than the steady gray eyes which watched him in return. Unlike many of the men in Magnus, Thomas kept his hair long. Tied back, it added strength to the impression immediately given through square shoulders, a high, intelligent forehead, and a straight, noble nose.

Thomas had spent the entire winter in Magnus learning

and practicing swordplay. The hall outside had rung again
and again each day with the clang of steel against steel, and
no man could handle a broad sword for hour after hour
without developing considerable bulk, a bulk shown in the
corded, muscular arms and chest now bare as he sat with the
blanket at his waist.

Muzzamar noted all of this, and not for the first time,
wondered what game these Europeans played so fearlessly
here in a land that had been lost to them a generation ago.

The shrieks and groans outside renewed in pitch.

The large man noticed Thomas lift an eyebrow in question.

"Camels," Muzzamar explained. "Evil beasts. Smelly, stub-
born, and evil. Put upon this earth only to try men's souls.
They will protest their load this soundly every morning until
we reach Damascus."

"Forgive my question, please," Thomas said softly. "Am I
not to travel to Nazareth?"

Unconsciously, as if to reassure himself, Thomas pressed
his leg against the sealed package beside him beneath the
blanket.

"Of course, of course," the man said. "From here, we travel
to the Valley of Jezreel. After several days passage through
the valley—near Mount Tibor—a road leads north to Nazareth. Some of my men will take you there as this caravan
continues east to Damascus. Did not your friend explain?"

"Sir William had time to explain little," Thomas said. "He
cautioned me to avoid soldiers who might inspect this caravan. He—"

"Good advice indeed," Muzzamar said quickly, "something
I cannot repeat enough. We travel in this land only by a pass
of safe conduct granted by the Mamelukes. That safe conduct
does not include passage for men from across the Great Sea.
Should you be discovered, I cannot vouch for your life."

Muzzamar gestured behind Thomas. "Those worthless servant girls left you clothes of the desert. The head veil will protect your face from sun and wind, of course, but also from curious Mameluke soldiers. You will travel among the slaves, but even so, be advised to wear it at all times."

Muzzamar paused, then said, "I should not worry overmuch about the soldiers, however. This caravan carries much wealth. On these roads, we face a much greater danger from bandits."

7

Thomas hardly noticed the passing of hours.

It had been a new experience, to be sure, his first moments atop the great two-humped beast. The camel had been on its knees until expert hands guided Thomas into the small saddle between its humps. Then the camel had awkwardly pushed itself up on those splayed legs until Thomas sat high above the ground. Infrequently, the camel had turned its massive head and snorted foul breath as it attempted to regard its new rider. But the slave trader traveling alongside Thomas had whipped the camel's neck upon each occasion, and now the camel contented itself with maintaining the pace of the caravan.

And, for the first few miles, Thomas had marveled at the serene smoothness of this method of transportation. Except for the pressure of the small saddle—which he knew would leave him sore by the end of the day—he felt as if he were floating far above the sands. And to think that these great beasts could go *days* without water.

Thomas had idly wondered if it would be practical to take camels back to England, and that had led to renewed memories of Magnus. Those memories—as time slipped by without his notice—had then led to his usual doubts and questions.

In the last few days at sea before reaching the Holy Land, Katherine had answered many of Thomas' questions—if her answers were to be trusted. The knight too had helped clear up some mysteries.

Even now, contemplating it for the thousandth time, Thomas felt an odd mixture of thrill and relief at his new-found knowledge. *He was a Merlin. One of those specially trained to battle against a secret circle of Druids.* That explained much of his childhood, much of the mystery behind Magnus, much of his precious books of knowledge. And much of the destiny given him by Sarah, his mother.

Each time that phrase—*Sarah, my mother*—entered his mind, Thomas forced it away with vigor. He would grieve, yes, but in privacy, not among the men of this caravan as it snaked slowly forward beneath the hot sun.

His new knowledge too explained much of what had happened at the gallows so long ago as he first embarked upon his quest to reconquer Magnus. Yet new questions still arose. *Who had the old man been, with the power among ruling men to arrange a hanging on the day and hour an eclipse would occur?*

Now Thomas was left to wonder about his *new* quest in this strange land—and the package he must guard so carefully.

Thomas felt dark suspicion too. Both Sir William and Katherine had said that the Merlins were unable to reveal themselves to Thomas because they were not certain of his loyalty. Their suspicion was simple but well-founded. It *was* possible that Druids—in the years following Sarah's death—might have converted Thomas to their evil ways. Sir William, Katherine, and the old man could not know that this was not so. So they withheld the answers he needed.

This matter of trust was important. Both the knight and Katherine had hinted that the Druids might—through Thomas—find the one secret they needed to end their centuries-old battle with the Merlins. *What was the secret they believed he held? And what terrible end to the battle might lie in store?*

His suspicions darkened more. *Having revealed so much, why would they not tell him all? Unless Katherine and Sir William did not yet trust him completely? And if Thomas was not yet trusted completely, why did they now reveal anything at all?*

In his confusion, Thomas groaned, loudly enough to draw attention from the rider nearby. So Thomas patted his belly, as if the groan had resulted from a poorly digested breakfast.

Then he returned to his thoughts. *If he was not yet trusted, why did they reveal anything?* A year ago Sir William had spent months in Magnus, with ample time to draw Thomas aside in privacy. Katherine too had many opportunities in Magnus to do the same. *Why did they give him answers now in St. Jean d'Acre, and not then?*

Thomas groaned again, and upon this groan, ignored any glances. Were the answers in the package entrusted to him? Not for the first time did he consider unsealing it.

No. Thomas repeated the arguments he had given himself. *Were Sir William and Katherine foes, they would have given him nothing that might benefit him. Were they friends, then unsealing the package would cost him their allegiance.*

Thomas closed his eyes briefly. *Should he in return trust them?* Enough strange events had occurred so he might full well believe *they* were Druids, determined to locate his treasure of priceless books.

His only choice was to play this game to its end. And now the bait promised him—if he were among enemies—was nothing less than the father he had long believed dead.

8

The caravan moved south along the flat road of the coastal plains. Far ahead high, rounded hills, blue with distant haze, shimmered against the backdrop of an almost white sky.

The heat seemed an attacker. Each time Thomas wiped his face and exposed his skin to the scorching air, he breathed gratitude at the layers of fine, light cloth which trapped cooler air close to his body. Long before the sun passed its highest point, one of the leather skin bags of water tied to his saddle was half empty.

Much more difficult than the heat for Thomas was the evil of watching the slaves stumble alongside the camels. There were a dozen; they too wore the layers of white for the desert heat, and they too had covered heads against the blazing white sun, for Muzzamar knew dead slaves were of little value in Damascus.

They were marked different, however, by the single rope which attached one to the other. This rope was looped around each neck, so that when one fell, he risked dragging the others down. When one slowed, he himself risked strangulation.

Thomas noted too the slaves had no skins of water, and he vowed to ease their thirst as soon as he could.

Muzzamar, at the front of the caravan, finally raised his sword to call a halt when the lead camels reached a stand of trees which hugged a wide well.

Thomas did not dismount until he had loosened two of his waterskins from the saddle.

He nearly fell when his feet first touched the packed sandy road. Sitting motionless for so long in the heat had cramped his legs, and it took effort to straighten them.

Thomas ignored the scowl of the slave master—for the heavy waterskins were obvious in his hands—and moved to the first of the slaves. He had been warned by both Sir William and Muzzamar not to draw attention to himself, but he knew the men on foot must be in agony.

"Take this," Thomas said as he held out the waterskin, "then pass it along."

The slave lifted his head. Dark eyes, glazed with exhaustion, now opened wide with surprise. The slave hesitated briefly, then snatched the leather bag from Thomas and gulped water.

Thomas waited, then realized the slave had no intention of ending his drink, so he gently grabbed the slave's wrists and pulled the waterskin away.

Thomas carried the waterskin to the next slave. While that slave drank, Thomas tried to ignore the obvious rope burns around the slave's neck.

Then to the next. And the next. Until he reached the last slave held by that rope, the terrible line of death.

Unlike the other slaves, this one did not open his hands gladly to receive the waterskin.

"Take this." Thomas urged the waterskin on the man.

"You risk your life," the slave answered, head still down.

Thomas stepped back in surprise. *The man had spoken English.*

"Among these nomads, it is considered a weakness to show mercy," the slave continued. "And we will be fed and watered at nightfall, for they have no wish to kill us as—"

"English," Thomas blurted in that language. "You speak English!"

The slave redirected his stare from the ground to Thomas, and the eyes which rose were not the deep brown of these darker people, but a blue so piercing it almost startled Thomas.

"I speak English because I am English," the man said in a low voice. "Find it not so amazing. Many of us are doomed in this strange land, the long forgotten of a forsaken Crusade. I avoided capture for ten years. Ahead. . . . "

The man shrugged. His face showed no expression. It was an older face of a man equal to Thomas in height. How old, Thomas could only guess, but as the wind tugged against the cloth which protected the man's head, Thomas saw edges of gray at the temples of the man's dark hair. The wrinkles around the man's mouth and eyes had not yet deepened enough to show shadow. His nose was crooked in several places, as if it had been broken more than once. What little of his teeth flashed during his quiet words showed them to be straight and without gaps—the man had not eaten poorly while he avoided capture.

"Ahead," the man finished, "lies what tomorrow brings."

Thomas again pushed the waterskin toward the slave. This time the water was accepted, with another shrug. The slave drank slowly, then returned the water.

"You are too young to have arrived with the last Crusaders," the man said. "Yet your command of their tongue tells me you are not a new arrival to this land. And you are not among us slaves. . . ."

Thomas recognized it as a statement, not a question, and simply nodded in reply.

"Your story must be one of interest," the man finished.

Again, the man spoke in neutral tones. Again, Thomas nodded.

"Do not attempt to help me escape," the man said calmly.

Said thus, an unexpected statement with the same lack of passion as all the man's other words, the advice had the impact of a physical blow. For indeed, Thomas was contemplating that same subject.

Before Thomas could protest, the man fixed him with those uncanny eyes and unhurriedly spoke more.

"We are fellow countrymen. And, me thinks, men of the same breed, for cowards and ne'er-do-wells would not stray across a world to enter the Holy Land." The man raised his voice slightly. "Yet do not offer your help. Even should you succeed, with me you would become a hunted outlaw with no place to hide."

A deep laugh greeted that remark.

"Well spoken, Lord Baldwin!" The words came from behind them in Arabic, for Muzzamar had approached quietly and unseen to Thomas. "Words spoken on my behalf?"

Muzzamar clapped Thomas on the back. "Lord Baldwin saw me, of course. But it is still advice worth heeding. For you are a stranger among us, and I suspect you know little of our history."

Muzzamar took Thomas by his elbow. "Come with me into the shade. For we have a little time before our journey resumes."

Thomas glanced at Lord Baldwin. The older man nodded

slightly, a gesture which seemed a farewell among equals.

Muzzamar spoke as he guided Thomas back to the trees. "You know, by now, of the Mamelukes. Two centuries ago they were slaves to the Egyptians. They overthrew their masters; later they overthrew the foreigners who built fortresses and castles all across this land."

The trader pointed east. "In those hills, as you might know, stood the great Crusader castles. The greatest, known as Saphet, commanded the very road we travel. The Mamelukes had laid siege to Saphet and promised safe passage to the knights upon their surrender. Yet when the gates of the castle were opened, every knight was beheaded upon the spot."

Muzzamar examined Thomas for his reaction.

"So you see," Muzzamar's smile was a caress of cruelty, "we cannot afford to anger the Mamelukes. To *our* enemies, we are equally ruthless. And neither we, nor the Mamelukes, show the softness of the English."

Muzzamar tapped the near-empty waterskin Thomas still held.

"We do not provide comfort to our enemies, and we show no mercy to those who betray us." Muzzamar's smile did not change as the implied threat continued. "Perhaps you feel duty-bound to help another, even at the cost of his own life. Take the advice offered by Lord Baldwin. Journey along your own path. I have guaranteed your safety because I have accepted gold. And I am no common bandit. I will deliver you as promised."

Muzzamar's voice then flattened with deadliness. "But should you become an enemy, you will have the choice of death or slavery. And death would be more pleasant."

9

On the eve of the third day of travel, Muzzamar visited Thomas in his tent.

"My young friend," Muzzamar beamed, "tonight, we shall feast."

"Even more?" Thomas said. He finished drying his face. It had felt wonderful to dip in the basin supplied by servant girls and wash away the day's dust and sweat. "Surely you cannot exceed the goat's milk curds and dried figs which have sustained us thus far."

Muzzamar frowned, then laughed with understanding. "A jest!"

With a return smile, Thomas nodded. A jest indeed, for the previous few days of travel had been at a forced pace. Tents had not been raised at nightfall, nor were cooking fires lit. Sleep had been short and in open air. The entire caravan had always been ready to move.

"Truly," Muzzamar said, "our people do not always eat in such a manner. And tonight, you shall taste our finest."

"No danger of bandits tonight?" Thomas asked. "Nor of Mameluke soldiers?"

"We are well into the Valley of Jezreel," Muzzamar said, as if this explained all.

"My apologies for ignorance," Thomas said. "You have been greatly occupied, and there was none other to inform me of matters of the journey."

"Of course, of course," Muzzamar said. "My own apologies for neglect of an honored guest. Yet we were in bandit-infested country, and my first duty was survival of the caravan."

"The hills on each side promised danger?" Thomas asked.

"Yes. The passage into this valley is well guarded by those hills. It favors large groups of bandits. Naturally, we are able to protect ourselves, but only at great cost, and to tarry in those hills provides the bandits unnecessary temptation. But now," Muzzamar swept his arms wide, "now we are in the open valley. And more so, a caravan of traders on its way to St. Jean d'Acre has joined us in its passing. There is safety away from the hills and safety in numbers, Thomas. We shall rest here and feast. You will be welcome at the feast, for it is hardly likely that Mameluke soldiers will appear at night to inspect the caravan."

"How long is the rest of my journey?" Thomas asked. For thoughts of Nazareth and Sir William and Katherine and his father filled his every waking moment.

"The road to your destination is only a day's travel," Muzzamar said. "Well within sight of Mount Tabor. From there, two of my men will guide you north into the hills to Nazareth."

Muzzamar caught the darkness of uncertainty that crossed Thomas' face. "Come, come, Thomas. Have no fears. We have successfully passed through the dangerous country. As a small group, you and my guides will easily avoid Mameluke soldiers on the road to Nazareth. Now your arrival there is a certainty."

Thomas forced a smile. For his fears had not been of arrival but of what might occur after.

Thomas groaned as he laid his head to rest. The sealed package he had sworn to guard for Sir William was wrapped in a blanket and served as his pillow.

How could he possibly sleep?

Muzzamar's promise of a feast had been only a hint of the actual events of the evening. There had been tambourine dancing by veiled girls, rich meats and sweets, and servants pouring wine and delivering food, all to ensure the feasters—men from both caravans—need only sit and eat. Thomas had gorged himself, urged on by a servant who, it seemed, tended only to him.

His stomach, overfilled with unaccustomed delicacies, rumbled threats of rebellion. Even as he finally drifted into sleep, Thomas tossed fitfully.

His dreams too gave him little rest.

Thomas stood upon a high hill, shrouded in gray mist. The mist swirled then cleared, and rays of sunshine broke through from behind him—sunshine that lit an entire city across the deep valley, so that the beams of light danced golden and silver on the curved towers tall above whitened square houses that spread in all directions along the plateau of the mountain.

From the city walls came a dark figure, small with distance. The figure slowly moved closer, then close enough so that Thomas could see it was a large man, yet the man's face was without feature.

The peace Thomas felt to behold this city of dreams began to disappear, and in its place arrived a trembling panic, panic which grew stronger as the figure approached, stronger as Thomas struggled to identify the man's face.

But the face was gray with mist, and Thomas moaned with a fear he could not explain.

"Thomas, my son," the figure called. Now the man was close enough so that Thomas could see the wrinkles of the dark cloth folded around the figure. But still, the face was featureless and gray.

"Thomas, my son," the stranger called again. "Are you a Merlin?"

Thomas tried to reply "Father," but he could not speak, his fear was so great. There was something so threatening about this stranger who claimed to be his father that Thomas tried to reach for the sword at his side, but his hands were powerless. He stood mute and frozen.

"Thomas! Are you a Merlin?"

The figure transformed into a dragon. Yet before Thomas could scream, the dragon became Sir William, swirling out of sudden mists with a sword upraised.

Thomas tried to lift his arm against the blow, and as the sword came down, there was a roar, for the sword had struck, not downward against Thomas, but behind him at a lion that now snarled defiance against death as blood ran from its severed throat.

As Thomas turned back to thank Sir William, he caught the scent of perfume. The knight was not there. Instead, it was Katherine, her hair a halo of brightness from the sun. She reached for Thomas and he sobbed with relief.

Her arms pulled him close and she kissed him and joy filled him; yet something was wrong. Her kiss was one of death, for now he could not breathe, and she would not pull away.

He struggled, trying to push her away, but his arms were still trapped at his side, and she only pressed harder.

Breath, find breath, for he must live. . . .

Thomas opened his eyes wide in panic. For a single heart-beat, he relaxed. It had only been a dream.

Yet he still could not breathe. And above him, a giant of a man blocked the flickering light of the tent lamp.

In the next heartbeat of awareness, he realized a heavy open hand pressed down upon his mouth and nostrils.

1 0

"**Silence or death,**" a voice whispered.

To fulfill that promise, the figure above placed the tip of a knife against Thomas' throat.

"Silence or death," the voice repeated. "Nod if you choose life."

Thomas nodded. The slightness of that movement proved the sharpness of the knife and the seriousness of the intruder; Thomas felt the knife's tip break skin.

The hand over his nose and mouth was removed.

Thomas drew breath, but slowly, for he did not want the intruder to consider a gasp to be unnecessary noise.

Several more heartbeats passed until the figure eased backward and the pressure of the knife left Thomas' throat. "We leave camp," the voice said. "You will not return. If we are caught, we both die."

Thomas nodded again and hoped his agreement would be visible in the dimness of the tent.

He dressed hurriedly, careful to place around his neck the

long strap which held his pouch of gold beneath his clothing. When ready moments later, Thomas reached for the sealed package that had served as his pillow, for even the threat of death did not take its importance from his mind.

"Do not forget your sword," the voice said, "for you shall travel alone and without friends."

Thomas took the sword, grateful that this stranger would not see it as a threat.

And why fight now? For if the stranger had meant harm, Thomas would already be dead in his sleep.

The stranger turned. Thomas followed.

They moved between the tents. Something seemed unnatural, and it did not take long for Thomas to understand. The camp did not stir with the slight movements of guards at night, the occasional scurrying of servant girls, the restless muttering of slaves in their tortured sleep. Only the grunts and stampings of the camels showed any life.

The stranger led Thomas away from the edge of the caravan. To their left was the camp of the other caravan, the traders headed for St. Jean d'Acre. This camp too was unnaturally still.

The stranger continued his steady pace away from the camps.

Thomas held his questions. When this large man in front of him indicated the silence could be broken, then Thomas would speak.

For five minutes they traveled.

The sky above was ebony, broken by brilliant diamonds of starlight. The moon was high and full and cast enough pale light for Thomas to see the outlines of the far hills.

Finally the figure stopped and turned. "It does not matter my name," the stranger said. "I was among the slaves. Yet we were not slaves. Rather bandits, biding our time."

"Band—"

The stranger held up his hand. "I have little time until my absence is discovered. What I can explain is this. It is well known that Muzzamar's caravan has many riches and is too well guarded for attack. Instead of raiding, we posed as slaves until Muzzamar believed himself safe. The cook was bribed before we departed St. Jean d'Acre, before we let ourselves be put into bondage. And this night? As planned long before, all of the food of the feast was drugged. It was great fortune that brought us the other caravan to be plundered as well."

The stranger smiled as a look of comprehension crossed Thomas' face. *Time and again his plate had been filled before he could rise to join Muzzamar and the others with their feasting. And each time his plate had been filled by a large slave.*

"Yes," the figure said as if reading Thomas' thoughts. "I ensured that you were kept from the food that all others ate. They sleep now. It was a simple matter for the cook to release us from our bonds and supply us with their very own weapons. It is an easy way for us to plunder, much simpler than open attack from the hills."

"Those weapons shall be used against them?" Thomas asked. "Many in camp are innocent women and children."

"Only the men shall die. This is a harsh land."

Thomas said nothing. He pondered the merits of attempting to warn Muzzamar. Yes, he had seen men die, but always in battle, not as helpless sheep.

"Your silence says much," the slave said. "Yet there is nothing you can do to prevent this. The men are heavily drugged, and your return will only ensure your death, and mine for assisting you now."

Thomas realized this was so. For a moment, wildness tempted him. To die, useless as his death might be, in attempting to warn others might prove to be a lesser evil than a haunting guilt later. But ahead was Katherine and Sir William and his father, and the fight of the Merlins.

"My own life has been spared." Thomas said it in an empty tone, as he tried to force his conflicting emotions aside.

"You gave us water," the slave answered Thomas. "And I have decided to repay you in kind. I wish I could give you a camel, but while your absence will be undiscovered in the confusion to come, the loss of a camel is too easily noticed. Our own leader is without mercy and cannot know you have been spared."

Thomas absorbed this information.

Others would die, and he was helpless against it. The stranger in front of him had risked his own life to save Thomas. The gift could not be discarded. Thomas must leave.

"Truly," Thomas said, "there is no way I can repay you."

"I have heard of the man who walked this land, the man you blue-eyes claim was the Son of God. Did he not say we are all brothers? And did you not prove it with kindness?"

The stranger extended his hand in a clasp of friendship. "Brother, may your God protect you. Shalom. Go in peace."

The stranger untied a full waterskin from his belt, handed it to Thomas, and stepped away. "You must reach the hills by daybreak. It will cost us both our lives for you to be found."

Thomas reached for the stranger's arm at a sudden memory of a brave and noble face. "The slave from my own land — Lord Baldwin?" Thomas asked. "Will he too be slain?"

The stranger snorted in irony. "During this journey, we have discovered the hell of slavery ourselves. All slaves in both caravans shall be spared and released."

Then a pause before the stranger spoke more soberly. "Whether he and they — like you — survive this land is an entirely different matter."

1 1

Thomas entered Nazareth at dawn. Behind him was three days of cautious travel—slow movement along the roads at night, sleep in shadows of safety during the day. Behind him lay the long and rolling hills of Galilee.

Among these hills grew forests of cedar and pine, olive orchards and vineyards, and fields with wheat and oats and barley. It had almost been a joy to contemplate the land as he rested hidden during the day.

Thomas was not thirsty. His waterskin was still half full from a well fifteen miles earlier, and travel during the night had spared him the searing daytime heat.

He was hungry, for he had not dared to stop at any inns or allowed himself to be seen during the day. Time and again Thomas had shifted his focus from his tightened belly to think of Nazareth. There he would reach Sir William and Katherine. There he would be in relative safety.

What if Sir William and Katherine had not survived their journey? Thomas dared not think of those consequences. For how then would he find his father?

No, he must trust the knight would arrive with Katherine. But Thomas would not be foolish as he waited. They might arrive in a day or a week, time enough for Thomas to be noticed by Mameluke soldiers or other assassins. Because of that Thomas had long ago decided he would satisfy his hunger, then find a place in Nazareth to wait, quiet and hidden as he surveyed arriving travelers.

A rooster's triumphant crow broke the silence of his thoughts. The dawn's light was still soft and the town ahead appeared motionless in the growing shadows.

Thomas chose a large boulder to use as support and leaned back to survey the buildings ahead. Nazareth seemed small and quiet and ordinary, hardly a place to be remembered by generations. Yet there was a timelessness about the town, its small flat buildings as ancient as the hills, and Thomas again let himself contemplate the awe of the burden of history that had given Nazareth and the rest of the Holy Land such significance in human matters.

It was in these moments that Thomas felt most at peace, when he believed he could feel the presence of the God of his fathers and forefathers, the God who had shown the very same presence to men of this Holy Land since the beginning of recorded time.

In these moments, Thomas lost himself in a quietness, as if he could hear the voices of this land reaching to him across the centuries. In this land Moses had climbed hills like these of Galilee to look across the Jordan River and fill his eyes with the awesome beauty of this Promised Land before the obedience of his death. Here, a great king named David had defeated invincible armies, and here David had sung psalms of praise and love. And here, in the very town Thomas now surveyed, a boy had played in the dust of the streets, inno-

cent then and later as the man named Christ who had allowed himself to die so cruelly on pieces of rough wood tied
together in the shape of a cross.

Thomas shivered, even as the sun warmed his back. There
was strength to be received during this contemplation, he
knew, and he closed his eyes in a prayer of thanks for his
safety and a plea for God's continued help.

That prayer led him to another vision, one of a scene far,
far away in a land he hoped to see again. There, a woman
had started every morning in a cold, bare room silhouetted
against the light of the rising sun with her head bowed in
prayer and a young boy at her side.

Thomas blinked back a tear. As that young boy, he had
barely understood Sarah's daily silence. In this moment as he
remembered, his hunger faded and he knew that now—after
his journey and before Katherine and Sir William might arrive in Nazareth—he could afford the luxury and demand of
grief. Some instinct told him he must perform his own farewell ceremony for the woman who had given him so much
in that faraway monastery so many years ago.

Thomas tightened his jaw to keep his face firm and
stepped away from the boulder to seek a path into the hills
above Nazareth.

Thomas sat on the edge of a rock near the top of the
highest hill overlooking Nazareth. Here enough of a breeze
flowed to cool him. It brought the bleating sounds of a flock
of sheep grazing on a neighboring hill. But for that, the hills
were silent.

Thomas closed his eyes, and remembered again Sarah.
How difficult to raise a boy, to love him as a son, yet not once—

even when facing death—let the boy know the teacher was also mother.

And the son, Thomas thought dispassionately, as if it were someone else who had been raised without knowing the woman had been his mother, *she must have borne the pain daily of knowing her son believed he was an orphan.*

At that thought, Thomas bit his lower lip. Memories returned—memories of the questions he had asked about his parents and of his anger at God for letting them die.

And month after month, Sarah had patiently taught him in the ways of Merlins, unable then to reveal to him his duty.

Duty. Duty that required Sarah to sacrifice her identity as mother, duty that had let her die so far from her husband, let her die without telling her son of her love for him.

Thomas bowed his head and prayed, grateful that his faith allowed him to see beyond life on earth—too short and often difficult—and allowed him to realize that the pattern of the universe was so great and beyond comprehension that all he could do is trust and live as well as possible. In the way that his mother had trusted and lived.

Thomas sat on the hill for two hours, holding the sadness without trying to deny it. His tears and his prayers were all that he could give to the memory of Sarah.

Then he stood. Ahead, he could give more to the same duty that had called his mother. For that, he would have to hide openly in Nazareth. He had already chosen the method for that.

He would bribe an innkeeper to give him a room and keep it secret. During the day, he would pose as a beggar at the town gates.

After two days of begging, Katherine and Sir William arrived at midmorning.

With them traveled the two Muslim assassins from St. Jean d'Acre who had vowed to kill Thomas.

1 2

His first reaction was stillness. Stillness of shock. Stillness of disbelief. And stillness of a rabbit frozen by the sudden appearance of a fox.

Do not betray your presence, Thomas told himself. *Behave as would any crippled beggar at the town gates.*

The beggars on each side of him tapped the sides of their clay bowls, so Thomas did the same with his. Yet though his body reacted with movement, his mind was numb.

This cannot be. Heat has caused my eyes to deceive me.

He stole another glance. On foot, Sir William led a mule on which sat Katherine, veiled from Muslim eyes. Beside Sir William walked two men whose faces were engraved in Thomas' mind. Only days earlier, these large men had pursued Thomas and Katherine through the street markets of St. Jean d'Acre. Only days earlier, they had forced Sir William to barricade the house and set it ablaze. *And now?*

Now they walked at ease with Sir William and Katherine. There was nothing to indicate strain or tension, nothing to indicate that Sir William and Katherine were captives.

Thomas raised his head again and noticed that Sir William's sword was still against his side. *No, if they were captives, Sir William would not be armed.*

The beggars around him moaned for pity in discreet and respectful low voices. Thomas did the same.

It warmed him little that Katherine insisted upon throwing tiny copper coins into each bowl. *This was the woman who now betrayed him.*

Thomas ducked his head as they passed by and silently nodded thanks for the coin thrown in his bowl. Did he imagine the scent of her perfume as dust stirred by the mule's feet settled again?

He wanted to rise, to roar in anger at the evil of their deceit. He wanted to rush Sir William, to seize his sword, and attack the knight and his assassin friends.

He did not.

There was trembling in his legs and dizziness in his head at such unexpected and colossal betrayal. *Lies. So much of what they had told him must now be lies.*

How could he have been fool enough to believe his father was still alive? How could he have been fool enough to believe the tales of Merlin and a destiny to fulfill? And how could he have been fool enough to believe the promise of love in Katherine's eyes?

Thomas could not rise because weakness of despair overwhelmed him. As the murmurs of their conversation faded, he still could not raise his head to watch.

He did not bother to wipe the tears which fell shiny onto the tiny copper coin in the bowl at his feet.

It was another hour before Thomas found the energy to grasp the cane at his side. *What to do next? Where to go?*

A castle he had once conquered in the land of his birth no longer belonged to him. He was friendless in a strange land, involved in a battle he did not understand, a battle he had not chosen or invited.

Yesterday, there had been hope. Hope of finding his father. Hope of returning triumphant to Magnus. Hope of a trust in Katherine that might lead to—he barely dared think it in his bitterness—a love to fill him with joy.

Today?

Today he must continue his disguise and now walk away from these town gates leaning on his cane as if crippled, lest the ones he once thought friends discover he was in Nazareth.

Today, he had nothing. No hope, no dreams.

Thomas hobbled several more steps. He did not know, or care, what he should do next.

For a moment anger flared, and he almost hurled the clay bowl from his hand. Only instinct kept him from drawing attention to himself in such a manner, so he stopped in front of another beggar, apart from the others nearer the town gate.

"Take this," Thomas mumbled. He leaned on his cane and offered the bowl to the seated beggar.

The beggar looked up with disbelief. "It contains copper!"

"Indeed," Thomas said. *Copper from the hands of a young woman whose beauty he knew would haunt him each time he closed his eyes. Would that it were so easy to give away the memories as the coin and bowl.*

The beggar's hands shook as he accepted the bowl. "This means another cake of pressed barley for my daughter," the beggar said with gratitude. "There are days when that seems a feast."

Thomas looked more closely at the beggar. He had a slight face and seemed in good health. "Why are you not nearer the gate?" Thomas asked. "Where more travelers pass by?"

"It takes much of the morning for me to make my way here," the beggar replied. "Others, who arrive early, take the prominent positions."

The beggar noticed the puzzled look which crossed Thomas' face and pointed downward to the shawl over his lap.

"I drag myself here on a blanket. My feet are useless," the beggar explained. "I was caught once in a grinding millstone several years after my wife died in childbirth. I cannot work, and . . ." A smile of delight crossed the beggar's face. " . . . and I must feed my daughter. She will grow soon to be as beautiful as my wife, and then a marriage will secure her future."

The beggar continued to smile. "You see? In our lives we all have precious gifts. Perhaps, my friend, you do not have a child to love, but you are able to walk with the help of a cane, while I cannot. And when you are not rich, even a small copper coin can deliver joy, does it not? My joy is in receiving and your joy is in giving."

"Yes," Thomas said. Despite the blackness upon him, he managed a snort of self-mocking laughter. "And to imagine. There are those in this world with strong bodies, full bellies, and pouches of gold who let themselves despair."

1 3

Thomas arrived safely at the inn and retreated to the silence of his small room. He placed his few belongings on a stool, then sat cross-legged on the floor with his back against the wall.

First, he tore open the package. A book. Inside the cover, there was mention of a reward. He would read it later. On the other pages, the references were written in Latin, and as he scanned it quickly, he noted mention of scholars in Jerusalem and unrelated notes about the history of the Holy Land and quests of Crusaders. There would be time to study it in detail later.

Thoughts tugged at him.

Why had Katherine brought the light near while he fought a supposedly unknown assailant? She should have stayed beside him, ready to help in the fight. Now it made sense. She *knew* it was Sir William and wanted the fight to end before either was hurt.

But why practice such deception?

Thomas answered his own question immediately. *What better way for a Druid to convince him of friendship than find a common enemy to fight — the supposed assassins. Then, give him the mysterious package with cryptic words that may or may not have significance to further assist the illusion of trust.*

In sudden rage and pain at the renewed thought of betrayal, Thomas slammed the floor with his open palm. The shock of impact sobered him quickly, and he turned his back on the luxury of anger and hatred.

He closed his eyes in thought. *Regard this as warfare.* There are two choices: attack or retreat. Either action, to be most effective, requires surprise. Yet it cannot be certain that the bribe to the innkeeper will ensure my presence here remains secret. Therefore, either action must be taken soon or surprise will be lost.

Attack? Decide what is risked. Decide what is gained if the attack is successful.

Risk? One person against four. Three of the four are skilled in the arts of death. The other, Katherine, is one — it pained Thomas to admit it to himself — he would hesitate to harm. That hesitation — if she wished him dead — would prove deadly.

Conclusion — the risk is great.

What could be gained? If defeated and captured, could Katherine and Sir William be forced to divulge secrets? Hardly, and there would be no reason to trust their answers. Even holding them ransom would yield little.

Retreat? Decide the difficulty. Decide what is gained.

How difficult? His presence was still unknown. Retreat, then, would be simple. In these vast tracts of land, it would be impossible to find him.

What could be gained? His life — if indeed they wanted him dead. But why did they not kill him in St. Jean d'Acre? Or

before that? They wanted more than his life. If he knew
what it was that they sought, then this battle would be easier
to fight.

Time. Retreat gained him time to seek answers.

Thomas did not shift, so intense were his thoughts. A small
lizard crept from a crack in the wall to within inches of his
feet, unaware that the large object above it was alive. In
equal fashion, Thomas remained oblivious to his quiet guest.

And what was it they sought from him? Exiled in a strange
land, where would he find answers to questions he barely
understood?

There were only two places to begin. St. Jean d'Acre was
one. There, he had been raised as a child. That much he
knew to be true, for those few moments in that now-burned
dwelling had flooded him with memories. Whatever else
Katherine and Sir William told him might be false, but he
could not deny a childhood spent in St. Jean d'Acre. Not
with those memories, not when he knew the language of this
land. Somewhere in St. Jean d'Acre, he would find someone
who knew something. The tiniest scrap of new knowledge
would lead him to another. And that to another.

It would be safer now in St. Jean d'Acre. After all, Katherine and Sir William would be in Nazareth, still waiting for
him. *With answers, Thomas could return, and play their game by
his rules.*

Or, instead of returning to Nazareth after St. Jean d'Acre,
Thomas could go next to Jerusalem. So much pointed to it.
The Holy City. Perhaps he could find answers there.

Thomas smiled a tight smile to the silence of the room. He
still had his life. He still had his health. His freedom. And
enough in gold to sustain the search.

Thomas rose quickly, a movement that scuttled the lizard
sideways to another dark crack in the wall.

"My little friend," Thomas said, "I pray that my own retreat serves me as well as yours did you."

It was a prayer much needed. For two days later, as Thomas traveled a road that narrowed between large rocks on each side, bandits attacked.

14

His first warning of the attack was a slight scuffle of leather against stone. Thomas looked over his shoulder and saw two men dropping from the top of a boulder, only thirty paces behind.

There was no mistaking their intent. Swords raised, scarred and dirty faces quiet with deadliness, they advanced toward him.

Thomas glanced ahead to determine his chances of escape.

There, four more bandits had stepped onto the road. Walls of rock blocked him on both sides.

More terrifying than upraised swords was their silence and slow, patient movement. These men had no need to bluff or bluster—their purpose was to profit from the victim's death, not to take satisfaction from toying with the victim's fear. More chilling was that these men had no need to waste energy through haste—their victim could not escape.

A part of Thomas' mind noted this objectively, just as it noted that he was their intended victim, a thought he could not prevent, a thought that brought to him a surge of adrenalin.

Another part of Thomas' mind noted the terrain and evaluated his chances. The road was one that wound downward from the hills of Galilee. The plains of the Valley of Jezreel were barely an hour ahead, but that fact helped Thomas little now. The huge boulders on each side of the road were smooth, too smooth to climb.

The bandits closed the circle on Thomas step by certain step.

Thomas drew his sword. *One against six.* His death was certain. Yet surrender, impossible. Thomas did not waste his breath with threats. He too had the silence of deadly intent.

He began to back against a boulder for the slight protection it offered, then saw a break in the rocks beyond the four men advancing on one side.

Use more than your sword, Thomas could hear the long ago words of Sir William as he had once coached him in the art of fighting. *Terrain, a man's character, and surprise are all added weapons.*

Even in this situation, the thought of Sir William and betrayal brought bitterness to the back of his throat. It brought anger too. Anger which Thomas could direct at these bandits. He dropped to his knees and without taking his eyes from the four men on his left, felt about for stones. He found two and stood.

Still silence from the bandits.

The two on his right were close enough that he could hear their breath quicken as they prepared to attack.

They expect me to attempt a break through the weakest part of their wall—the group of two, probably the stronger fighters.

So Thomas did the opposite.

He lunged at the four men on his left, and at the same

time threw both stones at head level. The bandits flinched and ducked, only for an instant, and the stones clattered on the boulder behind them.

But as they ducked, Thomas swung his sword in a vicious arc and plunged directly ahead.

The suddenness of his attack, the distraction of the stones, and the swiftness of his sword bought Thomas only a heart-beat of confusion.

It was enough to get him through their ranks.

Yet his intention was not to flee. What easier target than an open back? No, Thomas focused on the split rock ahead among the large boulders.

Was the split large enough?

Yes!

Thomas reached it only a step before the bandits.

He turned and faced them. Rock now protected him on three sides. The fourth side, open to the bandits, was wide enough to give him room to swing his sword, narrow enough to limit their attack.

The largest bandit spoke to the shadow which covered Thomas.

"Fool," he spat. "You think this saves you?"

Thomas did not reply.

"You only succeed in irritating us."

Thomas still said nothing, only kept his sword ready.

"Throw us your valuables, and we will leave."

For a moment, Thomas was tempted. Then he realized they would probably only retreat out of sight, and wait for him to reappear in the open. And even if he did survive, without his gold life in this strange land would be next to impossible.

So Thomas only stared at the bandit. The stalemate contin-ued for thirty seconds.

"Search the nearby hills," the leader of the bandits then called to his men without turning his head. "Find wood and dried brush."

Two of the men scrambled away from the road.

"You see," the bandit said, resuming his conversation with Thomas, "I have no intention of risking even one man in direct combat. Few travelers pass here, we have much time, and a fire will easily move you from your shelter."

The man's eyes narrowed. "I will promise you this. The longer you delay us, the longer it will take for you to die."

The bandit smiled faint amusement and began to whistle tunelessly.

Thomas wondered if this moment might be best to bolt from his shelter. With two bandits searching for wood, his odds were now only one against four.

The tuneless whistle continued.

Thomas noted the layers of scars across the bandit's forearms.

He has survived many fights.

Thomas noted the relaxed but ready stance of the other three bandits.

Neither are they strangers to battle. I will be killed. But better to die fighting than as a helpless captive?

Thomas did not have a chance to answer that question, for a short high buzz interrupted the tuneless whistle. And almost in the same moment, there was a light thud.

The bandit looked down at his right shoulder in disbelief at the crossbow arrow now buried in his flesh.

Another short high buzz. Another thud. And again a buzz and thud. Two bandits were down—alive and angry but unable to fight. The two other bandits were already running away.

"Thomas!" a voice called. "You are safe to join me!"

Spoken in English! And the unseen attacker knows my name.
Thomas stepped into the sunlight.

Above him, a dark silhouette rose at the top of a boulder.

Thomas ignored the two men moaning on the ground in front of him and took another step closer to the man with the crossbow.

The sun behind the man was bright, however, and much as Thomas squinted, he could not see the man's features.

The man dropped to the ground.

"During attack, always keep the sun at your back," the man instructed. "It gives you much light and blinds your opponents."

The man grinned and kicked aside one of the fallen bandits as he extended his right hand to Thomas in a weaponless clasp of friendship.

The voice and face belonged to the captured ex-Crusader Thomas had last seen struggling in the bonds of slavery alongside a caravan of camels. Lord Baldwin, the man who had warned him not to give water.

"Ah," Lord Baldwin laughed, "I see by your face that you *do* remember me. And I hope you will consider this a debt paid. The water you once offered a poor slave in return for your life now."

Thomas nodded, still barely able to comprehend the suddenness of Lord Baldwin's appearance and rescue.

"I've been following for some time now," Lord Baldwin said in response to Thomas' reaction. "Curious to see how you might react to danger."

The large wolfish grin flashed wide and white.

"Thomas," he said, "you are no coward. I propose we journey together."

1 5

KATHERINE
Nazareth: a Love Betrayed
LATE SUMMER A. D. 1313

Katherine wished that she had been born deaf. For then she could not have heard the words which now pierced her heart.

"Thomas has failed our test." The muscles around Sir William's eyes tightened as he spoke. "We must conclude he is not a Merlin."

The test. So long ago, it now seemed, she and Thomas had reached St. Jean d'Acre. And while he was in the public baths cleaning away the stench of weeks in the brig of the ship, she had slipped to the house she remembered from her youth, a house and location she had kept secret from Thomas. There, to her surprise and delight, Sir William had greeted her, and they had hurriedly devised a way to test whether Thomas was truly a Merlin. Two others of the cause— posing as assassins—would pretend an attempt on their lives as soon as she rejoined Thomas. Then—as did happen—they would escape fire into the tunnel while Thomas believed assassins lurked nearby. In this manner, Sir William and

Katherine could hurry Thomas into accepting the need for separate travel. In this way, they could give him something of pretended tremendous value. If he appeared in Nazareth, with the parcel still sealed, he could be trusted. If he did not appear. . . .

"Can we not wait one more day?" Katherine asked. "Perhaps Thomas has been delayed."

And, she added to herself, *to wait meant hope—any hope at all—that Thomas could be trusted and believed.*

Sir William resumed his pacing of the inn courtyard and did not reply immediately, as if he were indeed considering her request. The sun had long since passed the highest point of the day. As the air cooled, so had Nazareth quieted and settled. The calls and babble of the town market beyond the inn was now the silence of an early evening breeze which rustled the leaves of the courtyard's fig trees.

"No," Sir William finally said. "We have waited two weeks. Each day I too have told myself he has been delayed. But that is wishful thinking. We must force ourselves to accept the bitter truth. Thomas has deceived and betrayed us."

Katherine heard a tiny voice speak. "Mayhaps . . . mayhaps he is dead." She was startled to realize the tiny voice was hers.

How she was torn. For if Thomas were dead, there was the consolation that he had not betrayed them, and she could always love his memory. If he were alive, she would have to learn to hate him, even though she would always harbor the slightest hope that somehow he might be part of their cause and that her love for him could against all odds be realized.

"He is not dead," Sir William said. "No matter how much I might wish to use that for an explanation. You remember the package and how we prepared ourselves for that terrible event, do you not?"

"Yes," Katherine sighed. A great reward had been promised to the finder of the book inside the package entrusted to Thomas. If Thomas were killed by accident or murder and the package opened—for what passerby or murderer would not be curious about a sealed package—there would be found the message directing the finder to appear in Nazareth with the book to receive a great reward. Yes, should Thomas have been killed, or found dead along a road, someone would have appeared, or at the very least sent a messenger, to inquire about the reward.

"Must we make this decision?" Katherine continued in the same sad voice.

Sir William stopped his pacing, moved toward her, and placed his hands upon her shoulders.

"Katherine, even a blind man can see how deeply you feel for Thomas. I have delayed my decision until now simply because of that."

A single tear trickled down her cheek.

"He is a fool," Sir William said softly. "A fool to choose evil and a greater fool to walk away from your love. But that is his decision, and now we must make ours."

Katherine bowed her head and patted Sir William's right hand where it rested upon her shoulder. Then she wordlessly turned away and, head still bowed, began to move across the courtyard to her room in the inn.

The quietness and acceptance of her grief and pain was much more powerful than if she had protested in anger, and because of that, Sir William felt the urge to justify his decision.

He called to her back.

"Tell me again," he said, "of the trouble in England."

She paused.

He took three strides and guided her to a bench in the

corner of the courtyard. Deep purple had spread across the sky as the sun dropped behind the far hills, and already the brightest stars could be seen. Doves chuckled and cooed as they settled on the roofs of nearby buildings. For a moment, Katherine said nothing, and the peace of the evening fell upon them.

"England," she said, almost in a whisper, "tell you again of England?"

Sir William nodded.

So she said, "The old man is dead. And the Druids—once secret and hidden among the people—have conquered Magnus by posing as priests. They claim power through the legend of the Holy Grail and by demonstrating miracles which are false. Now, in a large circle outward from Magnus, in one town after the other, they slowly gain converts to their cause."

Sir William nodded again, then said abruptly, "Have you ever questioned *our* cause?"

The change of subject and change in his tone startled Katherine, and for a moment she was at a loss for words.

"You have never once questioned the sacrifices you have made to be one of us, a Merlin?" Sir William persisted. "Not during the years your face was hidden in bandages, and you had to live as an outcast so you could report the activities of Magnus to the old man? Not when other young women your age were dreaming of love and children? Not once did you question your role among us?"

"I . . . I. . . ."

"And now," Sir William pushed, "as I make the decision to turn our backs on the one you *do* love, now are you at peace to be a Merlin?"

Katherine drew a breath to sit tall and faced him squarely with the dignity of royalty.

"I question," she said. And waited.

"Good," Sir William said, "for a faith tested is a faith strengthened. And a faith unable to stand questions is a weak faith indeed. Here, now, I wish to answer your doubts."

He stared at the brightening stars as he searched for what he must say. "For your sake, I am glad mere words cannot describe the evil I have seen, the ways that Druids have killed men, how terrible their destruction of many of the best of us when they first conquered Magnus and forced us to flee England.

"Druid ceremonies involve the ritual murder of the innocent. They believe the death of that soul transfers life and fortune to the one they choose. This death? They place the innocent into a wicker basket and lower that basket into fire."

Sir William clenched his jaw at unwanted memories. He stood, paced, and sat again before he could continue.

"As you know, King Arthur's Merlin was once a Druid. His Druid knowledge of science and potions gave him seemingly magical powers among ordinary people. Then Merlin turned his back upon the Druids and founded Magnus all those centuries ago, an island castle in a remote corner of England. There he taught others the Druids' skills to be used against them. He sent these new *Merlins* throughout the country to combat the Druids in hidden warfare. That generation taught another generation to do the same, and that generation another, so that down through the centuries, the Druids could never reach their ultimate goal. Magnus served us—"

"I know this," Katherine said. "The story is told to each Merlin as he or she comes of age."

Sir William smiled. "It is important enough to repeat. And I want you to think of it as you force your heart away from Thomas."

The knight paused to remember his place in the story, then began again as if he had not been interrupted. "Magnus served us well. For hundreds of years, the Druids did not know of our existence, and time and again from secret positions in society, the Merlins defeated them. Even after the Druids finally discovered our purpose, they could not locate Magnus. And when they finally knew of the castle of Magnus, it took generations for them to conquer it, barely years before your birth. Their surprise attack and ruthless slaughter twenty years ago all but destroyed the Merlins. Only a few survived."

Sir William closed his eyes, fighting unwanted memories. When he spoke again, his voice was strained.

"You must understand, Katherine. Generations of us have sacrificed all to fight the Druids, a terrible battle hidden from the people. Now that Magnus has finally fallen, now that there are so few Merlins, the Druids boldly and openly begin to control the people. They now seek to complete the terrible act that the first Merlin fought to prevent by founding Magnus nearly eight hundred years ago."

"That act?" Katherine asked. "The old man always said I must not be burdened with the knowledge. But now the old man is dead, and it appears we fight alone."

Sir William searched her eyes and made his decision. "That act? You shall be told, although few of the Merlins are. And you shall be told as we travel to the Holy City, Jerusalem."

"What of Thomas?" Katherine asked.

"He holds the key to the battle," Sir William said. "And we were almost fools enough to tell him where lies the final door to be opened by that key. Only this test. . . ."

He slapped his thigh in frustration and anger. "What of Thomas? Tomorrow, when we travel, you will hear of the Druid evil. And then, like me, you will be able to bear the pain of the fate of Thomas."

Katherine pressed her hands to her face as the knight finished his anguished words.

"There are still knights of the Crusade in this land. They will be told. Thomas must be executed on sight. By sword or arrow, he must die."

1 6

They traveled on donkeys in a staggered line. Umar, one of the men who had posed as an assassin in St. Jean d'Acre, ranged the dusty road several hundred yards ahead of Katherine and Sir William. The other, Hadad, kept pace an equal distance behind. Both were alert for any signs of ambush and would cry warning at the first indication of a bandit attack.

It was not until they had departed from the high hills—so treacherous with hiding spots—and reached the road to Damascus in the Valley of Jezreel that Sir William felt relaxed enough to drop his constant search of the land around him and finally begin conversation.

"Soon enough," he said, "we reach the valley of the River Jordan. There, we will turn south and follow the river to Jericho. There, another road will take us high into the mountains of Jerusalem."

"You know a great deal of this land," Katherine replied. A breeze swept through the valley so that the travel was almost comfortable. Were it not for the hard saddle and the uneven gait of the donkey, Katherine might enjoy the journey, for in all directions the distant hills carved a hazy horizon against the pale blue sky. But even with physical comfort, her mind and heart would grieve for Thomas, and that clouded any joy she might feel in the freedom of the wide expanse of the valley.

"I know little," Sir William contradicted her with a smile. "What I know comes from talking with the two who guard and journey with us. Their families have served the Crusaders for generations."

Katherine was not sure that she wanted to discuss the matter which filled her with so much distress. Now that Sir William deemed conversation more appropriate than constant vigilance against bandit attacks, she wished to keep him from the subject of Thomas for as long as possible.

"Tell me," she then said, "how is it that knights of the Crusades still live in this land?"

Above them a hawk circled and screamed. Sir William glanced upward, and the tanned skin around his eyes crinkled as he squinted against the sun. He studied the hawk briefly, then grunted, "It does not scream from alarm but to frighten small animals into movement so that they become visible."

Then his shoulders relaxed and he faced her again. His blue eyes were serious as he studied her.

"For two hundred years," he began in response to her question, "the Crusaders fought and struggled to keep this land. Enough years that entire generations were born here. Indeed many were the noblemen who had the opportunity to return to the homelands of their fathers, yet they refused. The castles established here, after all, were their true homes.

"Then the Mamelukes finally swept the land, destroyed the castles and all the power of the Crusaders. For many who survived, it was impossible to return to Europe. For others, unthinkable. They began to wander the Holy Land, for as nomads they could avoid the Mameluke soldiers easily, much as we do now by traveling in a small group and dressed as the people who live here."

The hawk screamed again, and Sir William paused to watch in admiration as it dove in a magnificent rush. The hawk disappeared briefly in tall grass, struggled and flapped its massive wings, then rose again, screaming in frustration that its talons were empty.

"These knights are not Merlins," Katherine said.

"No," Sir William said. He understood the question behind her statement. "Would that there were now many of us to continue the fight. But we have no Magnus here in the Holy Land, no place to share the secrets and knowledge we use to combat the Druids."

He smiled again. "However, the knights recognize fellowship, and here among enemies they have learned to assist each other where possible. You might be surprised at how quickly news can travel from outpost to outpost, through messengers trusted by these knights. I, myself, have many friends among them—not Merlins, but good and capable men."

The conversation stopped and the silence between them weighed heavy. For both knew the other's thoughts. *Good and capable men now seeking Thomas for the purpose of his death.*

The donkeys swayed and plodded their sure steps for several more minutes before Katherine dared speak aloud her next question.

"Yesterday," she whispered, "you told me I would understand why Thomas must die."

And to herself she continued, *as if that is consolation for the pain I bear.*

Behind them the hawk screamed again, now a faint cry.

"I am certain you know much of the politics of men," Sir William said. "For the old man would have trained you as thoroughly as any Merlin in the old schools of Magnus."

Katherine nodded. *What was there in politics that the man she loved would so coldly betray her; what was there in politics that demanded the man she loved be sentenced to death?*

"There is also the politics of religion," Sir William said. "Something I wish were not so."

"Religion is a matter of God, is it not?" Katherine asked.

"I am not sure how Merlin himself might have explained it," Sir William said, "but these are my private thoughts."

Despite herself, and the dull pain of losing hope in Thomas that made her ache every moment, Katherine felt intrigued.

"I prefer to think of faith as separate from religion," Sir William explained. "Faith is God-made—the joy and peace He gives us with our belief in His eternal presence and with the belief in His promises to us. Faith, thus, is the private communication between God and each of us."

Katherine nodded. *For had she not spent many hours in prayer, had she not consoled herself countless times with such faith in her God?*

"Religion," the knight said, "religion is man-made. It is the necessary structure here on earth for men to learn and teach this personal faith. The church, then, though imparting the truths of God, is made and maintained by men. Church buildings are man-made; so is the structure of the religion. We have a pope who oversees bishops, who in turn oversee priests, who in turn oversee the common man."

Katherine nodded again.

"In this man-made structure of religion, there are many men of true faith. Thus, God ensures that faith is passed from generation to generation. Yet, because religion is of this earth and of men, it is flawed. Some men use the *structure* of religion for their own purposes and claim faith merely for the power it gives them within the structure. You have seen, I am sure, bishops fat and well-clothed while the ragged poor starve before them."

"Yes," Katherine said. "This troublesome fact leads many to doubt the truth in religion."

"Truth in *religion*. Is there truth in the stone walls of a church? No. The truth is in the contents of *faith*. One must look beyond the stone walls of the church to see it, just as one must look past the structure of religion." Sir William paused as he searched for words. "The fat greedy bishops are imperfect, but this does not mean the message they bring is equally imperfect. The structure in which God passes along faith is far from perfect, yet this does not mean the truth delivered by the structure is imperfect. Faith itself—the ultimate truths of God and His Son—is pure."

Katherine considered the knight's statements, then despite herself she laughed aloud, a laugh tinged with pain.

"I did not jest," Sir William protested.

"I find irony in a philosophical discussion while my heart grieves over the solid flesh loss of Thomas."

"Yet that is my point," the knight said softly. "Because of religion, Thomas and the Druids are deadly dangerous. Can you not see what might happen in England?"

Katherine said nothing in response. But her knuckles were white with tension as she waited.

Through the sham of false miracles, how long will it be before the Priests of the Holy Grail convince town after town to abandon one religion for another? How long until the priests of the Roman church are powerless?"

The knight closed his eyes as he spoke. "The king of En-

gland receives his power because the people believe he rules
by the authority of the Roman church and by the authority
of God. What then, when the people no longer believe in
that authority? What happens to the entire *nobility*, men ap-
pointed by the king to rule the nation?"

By his tone, these questions were not meant for reply, so
Katherine said nothing.

"It is not enough horror that the Druids plan to take from
the people their faith, they also plan to take total power
through devastation of the land."

"How?" Katherine asked.

"How? Through a method that Merlin could not abide, a
method that turned him against the Druids who raised him."

"How?" Katherine repeated.

"Do you remember the Earl of York? How generations of
his family followed the orders of any secret messenger who
showed the ring of the Druid symbol?"

Katherine nodded. She had been told the story by the Earl
himself, from his place of imprisonment—a dungeon in the
town he had once ruled.

"Do you remember what happened to the one ancestor
who did not obey a messenger's commands?"

Katherine frowned in thought, then said, "the Earl spoke
of a curse which killed his great-great-great-grandfather."

"Yes. Worms consumed that ruler's body. Legend tells of
his screams echoing throughout the castle."

Sir William clenched his teeth. "The Druids have a simple
method to cause a mysterious death. A potion they use
causes deep sleep and allows an evil one to dab honey in a
man's ears, then small maggots are dropped within."

Katherine's stomach turned at the thought of the painful,
prolonged death which would follow.

"Yes," Sir William gritted in response to her reaction. "Evil horror." He took a deep breath. "Katherine, imagine this. The masses of people begin to believe the Priests of the Holy Grail. And at the slightest sign of rebellion, the firstborn of every family dies such a death. Mayhaps even before rebellion, the firstborn of the rulers die in such a way. No man would resist. England would be theirs."

He clenched his fists. "Our Merlin education gives us the history of mankind. Five hundred years of dark ages have passed, dark ages when knowledge was scarce and all people held in chains by ignorance. Only now has the light begun to appear. Advances in medicine and science are upon us, and through the written word, are shared from man to man, country to country. Mankind now begins to advance!"

Sir William stopped to draw another breath. His voice was urgent. "Katherine, there may come the day when fair laws protect every man, when abundance of food and medicine lets a common man live to be forty, yes, even fifty years of age! When it will be common to read, so that all receive the pleasure you and I do from books! When because ignorance is no more, leaders of men must respond to the will of the people! This day may someday arrive, even if it takes generations after you and I have left this earth. A day when such abundance and ease of living causes nations to exist in peace."

Katherine found herself holding her breath to listen to Sir William's passion.

He stopped suddenly, then dropped his voice. "If the Druids conquer and begin to rule, they will bar the people from knowledge, for their own power is derived from the ignorance of the people. They will end this slow progress that has been made by the learned men of our country. And these ages of darkness—" he faltered, "these ages of darkness will be upon mankind for centuries more."

After five days, the small group of travelers reached the town walls of Jericho. The gatekeeper gave them only a passing glance; Katherine had veiled her face as was custom for all women in public, knowing it served another purpose, to hide her striking and unusual blond hair.

Once through the town walls, she noted that the streets were extremely narrow and ran crookedly in all directions. She passed the observation on to Sir William.

"Defense," he said. "Should invaders ever break through the town gates, they face the confusion of the twisting streets. Not only that, but streets this narrow force armies to advance in a column only four or five men wide. Thus, four or five defenders can halt the entire army, for those behind the leading ranks of the army are unable to fight. And—" Sir William gestured upward at the sun-bleached square buildings "—while the army is slowed on the ground, defenders up top cast down rocks or boiling oil."

Katherine nodded understanding, and then, as custom dictated for women, followed meekly behind Sir William and the other two men as they searched for an inn.

At dusk, with a lighted candle in his hand, Sir William moved to the opening cut in the blocks of stone that served as a window.

The fading afternoon sun cast a small shaft of light into the cramped room, light almost completely blocked as the knight stood in front of the window.

The walls were gray with years of accumulated filth. The room was completely bare except for a pile of straw in one corner. Beside the straw sat a pitcher of water and a bowl with figs and bread.

Earlier Katherine had dropped her blanket on the straw, then jumped slightly as two rats scurried out beneath her feet to dart to the wall and scrabble up to the window before disappearing. That surprise had not deterred her in the slightest, so eager was she to sleep on something softer than cold, hard ground.

"This inn is known to many of the forsaken knights as a safe haven," Sir William explained from the window. "Even so, I prefer not to have you sleep alone. The four of us shall share this room."

"That too sets my mind at ease," she answered. She twisted her head in efforts to determine Sir William's actions by the window. "And for one night, it is no discomfort to be guarded in such a manner."

Sir William stepped back. Three lighted candles were now standing in the window.

"It may be more than one night," he said. "For now we wait until this signal is answered."

The knock on the door came during the second night.

It was a soft knock, yet enough to pull Katherine from deep sleep. She sat quickly, and when Sir William opened the door, her eyes were clear and she was alert.

The three candles which burned on the windowsill cast unsteady light across the room.

The man who slipped inside the door wore the long flowing clothing of a desert nomad. As the door shut, he pulled the wraps from his headband and rubbed his hair lightly, as if relieved to be free of its restrictions.

Katherine watched him with mild curiosity. In the flickering light, his features were blurred, but not so much that she could not distinguish a flash of white teeth as he smiled greeting to Sir William.

The two men were of same height and build. The man's hair was dark, unlike the complexion of his skin, and his first words confirmed Katherine's immediate guess. The man was not a native to this land but rather of Europe, for he spoke in slow and measured English.

"I had despaired you might never arrive," the man said. "It was with great relief that I saw your signal in the window."

The man glanced around the room, and nodded at the two other men, Umar and Hadad. His eyes stopped on Katherine.

"Do my eyes mock me?" he said. "Or is this truly a vision of beauty?

Katherine nodded in return. She did not know this man and did not want to encourage him. But the voice was deep and smooth, and she admitted to herself that few women would resent words of charm from a man who carried himself so nobly.

"Your eyes do not mock you," Sir William said. He stepped between the man and Katherine to make introduction.

Katherine took the cue and rose.

As the man stepped closer, she saw that his hair was tinged with gray at the temples. *A handsome man, indeed,* she thought. Another part of her mind noted sadly that, handsome as he was, her mind could not release a vision of Thomas.

"This, sir, is Katherine. She is one of us."

So the man was a Merlin.

The man took Katherine's hand, bowed, and lightly touched his lips against the back of her hand.

"I am honored," he said.

Katherine raised her eyebrows in question, and Sir William answered immediately.

"This, m'lady, is a man with vast knowledge of the Holy Land, and as one of England's greatest knights, he has proven to be a great thorn in the side of the Mameluke soldiers who have attempted his capture for years."

"I am equally honored," Katherine said. "It is a pleasure to make your acquaintance, Sir . . . Sir. . . ."

Sir William quickly spoke again. "Lord Baldwin, Katherine. None other than Lord Hubert Baldwin."

"May we speak freely?" Lord Baldwin asked.

Sir William glanced at Umar and Hadad and spoke rapid words in their native language. They nodded in reply.

Then Sir William spoke to Lord Baldwin. "They will not resent it if you speak in English, a tongue they do not understand."

"And the lady Katherine?"

"She has proven herself repeatedly, Lord Baldwin. Now with so few of us in these desperate times, she must be counted among our Merlin leaders."

High praise indeed. Katherine hoped her flush would not be visible in the candlelight.

Lord Baldwin smiled broadly at Katherine. His teeth gleamed like a wolf's. Katherine tried to dismiss the thought, but failed. *A wolf—fascinating but deadly—what secrets might such a man carry?* His words interrupted her thoughts.

"I have heard the news, of course," Lord Baldwin said. "The one known as Thomas must be killed. And it should not be difficult to find him. Not when he is a stranger among the people of this land."

Katherine flinched but forced her face to remain as stone.

"But I know little else," Lord Baldwin said. "Why must he be killed? Did he not reconquer Magnus? Was not his father the—"

"Yes, yes," Sir William said quickly, as if he wanted to spare Katherine the pain of more thoughts of Thomas' betrayal. "Katherine, perhaps you might describe all that has happened since I departed from Magnus."

Katherine took a deep breath. "The situation in England is thus...." She repeated what she had told Sir William earlier.

Lord Baldwin's frown deepened at each new piece of information. "What can we do first?" he asked when Katherine finished.

Sir William grinned. "Listen to the man," he said. "He says the word 'first'. He believes something can be done!"

Then Sir William sobered. "I too have news from England." He faced Katherine. "I withheld it from you because I believed it unfair to give you false hope. I did not know if Lord Baldwin would reach us. But now that the one knight we need is here...."

"Spare the flattery," Lord Baldwin growled. "Tell us what you have."

"A letter," Sir William said. He hesitated. "From the old man himself. Given to a trusted messenger who delivered it to me in St. Jean d'Acre after months of journey from France."

Sir William looked to Lord Baldwin. "It arrived barely a week before Katherine did. I had no time to send you word and inform you of its contents."

Lord Baldwin dismissed the apology with a wave. "I am here now," he said. "That is what matters."

Katherine barely heard as she again forced her face to be stone. *The letter, then, was sent before the old man's death.* She remembered well her entire winter in France, how she had spent hour after hour in the library of the royal palace, wondering where the old man might be during his six-month absence.

Sir William answered her thoughts. "In the letter, the old man explains that he spent months traveling from monastery to monastery."

Searching for what?

Again, Sir William answered her thoughts. He reached for his travel pouch and withdrew a strange pale material, folded flat into a small square.

Puzzlement at the material was as clear on Lord Baldwin's face as on Katherine's.

"It is called paper," Sir William explained. "Much lighter and more pliable than parchment. The messenger informed me that all of Europe is now learning of its use from the Spaniards."

He handed it to Katherine. Gently, hesitantly, she unfolded it. *So much lighter than parchment,* she marveled. *And it does not crack to be folded.*

Almost immediately, however, her thoughts turned to the old man. For there, even in the low light, she saw his clear, strong handwriting.

"Read it aloud," Sir William urged.

She did so, in low, almost hushed tones.

From Paris this 3rd day of March, in the Year of Our Lord 1313—Word has reached me, William, that matters in Magnus are worsening. Our enemies have openly begun their final campaign. In less than two years from now, I fear, they will have gained enough power among the people to succeed.

William, we are yet unable to trust Thomas. Our friend Gervase is still in Magnus and watches carefully, but from him I have received no word that Thomas is one of us. And without trust in Thomas, we cannot be sure we will regain Magnus. Without Magnus, our efforts in England will be doomed.

Katherine closed her eyes briefly. Bitter sadness took her breath away. *The old man had been alive then. Gervase too. Thomas had yet to betray them both. It had been a time of hope. Now. . . .*

"Katherine?" It was Sir William's voice, gentle and worried.

She smiled a tight smile, and turned back to the letter, reading with a steadiness she did not feel.

Yet, even if England is lost to us, William, do not despair. It was no coincidence that we chose to flee to Jean d'Acre when Magnus first fell. While it has been commonly believed among us that retreat to the Holy Land was because of the crusading knights who might be of service, there is another, more compelling reason, one known only to the leaders of each generation of Merlins. This reason forced me these last months to travel to the ancient libraries of Europe, and I must pass it on to you in this letter, because should I die, the secret must not die with me.

Why not impart it to Katherine, you may ask. Simply because I cannot burden her with it. If there comes a time that I trust Thomas, he will be directed to the Holy Land.

Again, Katherine stopped. This time, however, she blurted

her thoughts. "The old man *did* direct Thomas here! How could he have trusted—"

Sir William placed a finger to his lips, a mild way to silence her. "Still, the old man was not certain, for he did not give Thomas what remains for you to read."

Katherine accepted the reproof and bowed her head to the letter.

Our founder Merlin knew only little of what lies hidden in the Holy Land, for the legend of it began more than three hundred years before his birth, a time when Roman generals ruled Britain.

Even then, hundreds of years before Merlin's birth, the Druids had long been hidden among the people, suppressed by the Roman conquerors of ancient Britain. Yet—as we know too well—the Druids retained considerable power and influence through total secrecy.

A story was passed from Druid generation to Druid generation about the Roman general Julius Severus, who ruled Britain some hundred years after the death of Christ. This general discovered the Druid circle but did not expose it. To let Rome know of the Druids would also let Rome know of their wealth and almost magical powers. Instead, Severus plundered the Druids in one fell swoop, taking a great fortune in gold and the book of their most valued secrets of potions and deception.

Much of the details was lost through the centuries, but what Merlin knew was that Severus was summoned from Britain to quell a revolt: a Jewish revolt in the land of Christ. Severus could not trust his treasure to be left behind, so he arranged to take it with him.

That is all the Druids knew, for they were not sea-

men and had no way of following the Roman general
and his troops across half a world. That too then was all
that Merlin knew, all that he could pass to the one he
chose to lead the next generation of his followers.

Yet the Merlin leaders of each new generation were
not idle. They anticipated the day that Magnus might
fall, and each generation was given the task of adding
to our scant knowledge of the stolen Druid wealth and
secrets. When the Holy Land opened to the Crusaders,
we sent Merlins here to search. Their notes are in the
book you received with this letter.

Katherine stared at Sir William. "This book. . . ."
"The one Thomas carried," Sir William confirmed. "Important enough for him to trust us if delivered. Yet without this
letter, meaningless."
Katherine nodded. She began to read faster, anxious to
know the contents of the letter.

William, I too have been given the task of adding to
that knowledge. There has been little to glean, even
among the best libraries of our civilization, for history
has too often been lost through the age of darkness, lost
or converted to legend. What I know now, however,
may be enough after these hundreds of years of mystery.

In the land of the Franks, I stumbled across a parchment which copied the words of the Roman historian
Cassius Dio, who wrote a brief notice of Julius Severus
and his war against the Jews. The Romans destroyed
nearly a thousand Jewish villages, and a half million
were slain. The Jewish rebels were finally defeated in
their last refuge—caves in the Judean desert, north of
the Dead Sea.

Severus—Cassius Dio writes—was recalled to Rome almost immediately after his victory in the Holy Land. It would seem unlikely he would take his treasure with him, for discovery of it by Roman officials would mean his death. Shortly after arriving in Rome, he died of sudden illness, taking his secret to the grave.

Yet there remains a peculiar fact noted by Cassius Dio. During one skirmish against the Jews near these caves, General Julius Severus lost 20 men in battle—against a handful of unarmed rebels. These 20 men, Severus reported, died as a portion of the cave collapsed upon them, and their bodies could not be recovered.

Surely it is more likely that these were the 20 men who transported the treasure, for wealth that great would take such assistance. And is it not likely that that the surest way for Julius Severus to guard his secret would be to kill those 20, in the cave where the treasure was buried? I believe so, and upon this now rest our hopes. Look to your friends in Jerusalem for guidance on the location of these caves.

Should Magnus be lost to us, and should you be able to recover what was so precious to the Druids, the wealth and their ancient secrets may be used against them upon your return to England.

I pray this letter finds you in good health, and that the Lord God be with us as we fight His enemies.

Katherine noticed her fingers were trembling as she finished the letter. She looked up to a thoughtful expression on Sir William's face and one of eagerness on Lord Baldwin's.

"I have heard rumors of the caves of refuge!" Lord Baldwin said quickly. "But I have always discounted them as myths, for stories were told of entire families living for months inside the earth. Yet this letter!"

Sir William pursed his lips. "You will assist us in the search?"

"To my death," Lord Baldwin said. He fumbled with a wineskin which hung from his belt. "And let us drink to this new hope!"

Sir William found the crude goblets supplied with the room.

Lord Baldwin insisted that Umar and Hadad join with them in the toast.

The wine tasted bittersweet to Katherine. But she had only a short time to give it thought, for immediately she became drowsy.

Odd, she thought, *I was not tired, not with such important news.*

Struggle as she might, her lips would not do her bidding, and she could not voice those thoughts to Sir William. Instead, she sat heavily, then collapsed into a stupor of wild dreams, among them that she had opened her eyes to kiss Thomas. She knew them to be wild dreams, however, for when she woke in the morning, she was bound and tied with rough hemp rope.

1 9

"Fools!"

Katherine struggled to sit so that she could turn to identify the speaker. It took her several seconds. Even as her mind was on the words, she was conscious of the terrible taste in her mouth, the thickness of her tongue, and the pounding of blood in her head that hurt as badly as the rope tight around her hands and feet.

"Ah, she wakes." The same voice continued, cruel and taunting.

Katherine, now in an upright position, swung sideways to prop her back against the wall.

The other captives—Sir William, Umar, and Hadad—were as securely bound as she. And sitting on the stool before the door was a man she recognized immediately.

Waleran. The spy who had shared a dungeon with Thomas so long ago, when Katherine had been a visitor disguised in bandages and Thomas was an orphan determined to win a kingdom.

"Did you sleep like a princess?" Waleran asked. His black eyes gleamed with smugness.

Katherine felt dirty under his leering gaze. He was an ugly man with a half-balding forehead above cheeks rounded like those of a well-stuffed chipmunk. Waleran's ears were lumpy and thick, so large they almost flapped, and his hair fell scraggly and greasy onto sloped shoulders.

She refused to satisfy him with a reaction to his biting words. She merely settled against the wall and waited.

"You can release her. She is not one of us," Sir William said thickly, "but merely the daughter of a knight. One to whom I have pledged safe passage across this land."

Waleran laughed. A short, harsh, mocking sound.

"Do you play me for as big a fool as you? She has spent time with Thomas, that I know from my spies."

Sir William swallowed hard, trying to work moisture into his mouth. "Thomas, as did I, served as escort. She knows nothing of his hidden reasons for remaining with her on the voyage to this land."

Another snort of laughter. "Fool. I was there in York when she entered the prison to speak to the Earl. She has been involved since the beginning."

Waleran watched Katherine's face. "It was like stealing from a blind beggar," he said, "arranging to let Thomas escape York with Isabelle and the cup of the Holy Grail." A frown darkened his face. "Though we have yet to recover the Grail."

In spite of her determination to remain silent, a greater need brought words to Katherine's mouth, for in the passing of a heartbeat, she had gained hope that Thomas was not a Druid, and she could not quench her love. "You arranged for Thomas to escape?"

"Are we so clumsy that he could march into a castle and

steal from us in broad daylight? The entire matter was prear-
ranged. From my cell beside the Earl's, I heard every word.
While you spoke to the Earl, I made certain that all knew
Thomas would shortly arrive at the castle."

Waleran smiled. It made Katherine think of flies crawling
across the face of a corpse.

"Had I known, of course," Waleran said, "that you were
with the old man, I would have had you arrested right there
in the prison. It would have saved all the effort of finding a
way to ensure Thomas would lead us to you."

Katherine's mind flew back to that afternoon in England,
and much suddenly became clear. Thomas had been the bait
to bring the old man into the open. Waleran had only needed to let Thomas *think* he had triumphed, then follow. Except
Thomas had not led the Druids' soldiers to the old man; the
old man had followed Thomas, so that the result was the
same: capture the next morning and the old man's death.

She spoke her thoughts, now dreading the answer.
"Thomas is not a Druid."

"Hardly. Were it so, I would not have taken such pains to
trace his every step across the world."

Her heart rose in joy. Then fell in defeat. For Sir William
had passed a death sentence on Thomas. Now, unless they
escaped, word could not be sent to end the sentence. And
every hour in captivity was another hour closer to his death.
He would die not knowing that she loved him.

"Waleran has been kind enough to explain," Sir William
said to Katherine. "Although if your head pounds like mine,
you hardly need to hear the name of the one who did betray
us."

The wine. Lord Baldwin.

"Betrayal!" Waleran threw his head back and laughed.
"This is a touching tale of woe. Thomas was waiting for you

in Nazareth. Disguised as a beggar. He saw you with your two friends and assumed you had betrayed him."

Not only would Thomas die unaware of her love, he would die believing she had betrayed him. Pain slammed her like a physical blow.

"How do you know of this!" Katherine demanded sharply. Too sharply.

"Ahh," Waleran said, his voice now like oil. "Concern? A concern of love? This knowledge may prove to be of use."

He steepled his fingers beneath his chin and stared at Katherine. "My dear, it is simple. Lord Baldwin was not away from St. Jean d'Acre, as Sir William believed, but nearby. Word of your arrival was immediate, and once he had followed you to the house and witnessed your carefully acted assassination attempt, it was an easy matter for him to anticipate the use of the tunnel, for as a Merlin, he too knew of it. Lord Baldwin then followed you and Thomas to the caravan. He needed only to bribe the caravan leader to let him travel as a slave. From this position, he stayed with Thomas and later, as he tells me, managed to find a way to earn Thomas' trust."

Katherine looked to Sir William. The knight closed his eyes and nodded. "You remember the hints we gave Thomas of a great secret? Lord Baldwin deduced from Thomas that our final destination was Jerusalem. As one of the forsaken Crusaders, Lord Baldwin, of course, knew of the safe house in Jericho. He convinced Thomas to journey with him to Jericho, then to Jerusalem. Here in Jericho, Lord Baldwin suggested a rest and hoped we might arrive soon. When he saw our signal, he prepared the wine on the advice of this man."

Waleran responded to the pointed finger of Sir William with a bow. "Through Lord Baldwin and messengers, I have been informed of every single step Thomas took. Child's play, to anticipate your arrival here and arrange for the drugged wine. And what an unexpected and superb catch, that Lord Baldwin might also take possession of the letter you so stupidly revealed last night."

"And now?" Katherine asked. The letter was not on her mind. "Where is Thomas now?"

Waleran shook his head in mock disgust. "Such fools. Can you not see the obvious?"

Katherine kept her gaze steady.

"Lord Baldwin has returned to Thomas," came the reply. "He has stolen a pendant from Sir William and will use that as proof that he is Thomas' father."

Waleran smiled another smile that brought a shudder to Katherine. "You see, my child, because of your blunder last night, we now know of the Salt Sea caves. Lord Baldwin will lead Thomas there as further proof that he is not a Druid. With that trust established, they will return to England. And Thomas will finally give us what we seek there. With our treasure restored, and with the final key to our plan, our victory will be complete."

The smile became a grimace of victory that almost appeared to be a death mask shiny across Waleran's face and skull.

"Once triumph is assured, three things will happen, my child. You and the knight will die, for there will no longer be a reason to hold you as hostage."

Two more heartbeats passed before Waleran spoke again.

"Thomas too shall die. And England will be ours."

20

THOMAS
The Dead Sea: The Final Test

LATE SUMMER A. D. 1313

"Did a slave girl strike your fancy?" Lord Baldwin asked Thomas. "I feared you might never return from the market."

Thomas shook his head no. *A slave girl? When the scent and vision of Katherine fills my heart in dreams by day or night?*

Despite his thoughts, Thomas returned Lord Baldwin's smile. There was no need to burden another man with his own grief.

"Not a slave girl. Merely sweets to sustain us on our journey." Thomas held up a small square wrapped in cloth. "Combs of honey. For if we depart Jericho today, I would not refuse small comforts along our journey."

Thomas grinned wryly at the small room around them. "Not that this is the height of princely luxury."

Lord Baldwin nodded agreement and began to lift his travel bag. "Our donkeys await at the stable," he told Thomas. "And our journey is long."

They had barely traveled five miles before reaching the portion of the road that climbed the hills toward Jerusalem. Dust already caked Thomas, for fellow travelers were frequent, and there had been little rain to make the soil of the road heavy.

Without warning, the donkey beneath Thomas stumbled. Thomas pitched sideways but twisted with a quickness that brought his feet below him fast enough to land standing.

Lord Baldwin chuckled approval. "Well, done . . . son."

Thomas stopped dusting himself with frozen abruptness.

"Yes," Lord Baldwin answered the stare of amazement. "Son."

Thomas straightened. "You . . . you are my father?"

"Just as you are a Merlin." Lord Baldwin dug beneath the layers of clothes that protected him from the heat. "This is the pendant that I have waited years to bestow upon you."

His words were so unexpected that Thomas ignored the donkey as it sagged back to sit upon its hind legs. He reached for the offered pendant.

He studied it carefully, aware that Lord Baldwin's eyes were intent upon him. The delicate carvings in the pendant showed a sword stuck in a stone, with the silhouette of the castle of Magnus in the background.

"You . . . you are my father?" Though the words were repeated, his tone was not startled disbelief but questioning hope.

"It was not by chance that I was able to rescue you from those bandits outside of Nazareth," Lord Baldwin said. "Nor chance that I was part of the caravan which accompanied you away from St. Jean d'Acre."

Lord Baldwin shook his head. "It was a cause worth my while, to be with you, yet I pray I need never be a slave again."

"You followed me?" Thomas said.

Lord Baldwin nodded. "I dared not reveal myself. Not in St. Jean. Not in Nazareth. Not with that treacherous Sir William nearby. It would have been a fight to the death, and too much is at stake for me to risk such an end. Not when I couldn't tru—"

Thomas tilted his head in quizzical amusement. "Not when you couldn't trust me." Thomas paused. "Why now? Why choose this time to tell me?"

"Because—" Lord Baldwin had no choice but to stop as the donkey groaned in pain.

Thomas scanned the road behind him, as if measuring the distance back to Jericho.

"Is this usual for such a beast?" Thomas asked, then mused. "At least we are within sight of the town. It is not too late to turn back and find another donkey should this one prove to be seriously ill."

"I confess this matter *is* puzzling." Lord Baldwin frowned as the donkey groaned again. "Never in this land have I seen a donkey behave so."

"Shall we wait?" Thomas suggested. "Perhaps the beast has indigestion. If we rest in the shade, it may recover. . . ."

Lord Baldwin nodded, so Thomas hobbled both donkeys, reached for a pouch which hung from the donkey's saddle, and grabbed it before climbing rocks which led away from the road. After the climb, he stopped in the shade of a large boulder and waited for Lord Baldwin to sit beside him.

It gave them a view of the entire valley, and far away Thomas saw, or perhaps imagined he saw, the green ribbon of trees that lined the River Jordan.

"*Father*," Thomas said as he tried the strange word. "*Father*. It is strange. I do not know how to feel."

An ironic smile from Lord Baldwin. "Merlins are trained to

know so much, but this is something even the best teacher could not anticipate."

Thomas stared at him. "You know of Merlins. You call Sir William and Katherine by name, though I had only told you that two friends betrayed me. I cannot doubt you are my father."

"We will have much to share, my son." Lord Baldwin slapped Thomas on the back and smiled his handsome wolfish smile. "Much to share."

Thomas opened his travel pouch and unwrapped a comb of honey which he offered to Lord Baldwin. The older man bit into the sweetness with an eagerness that prevented him from speaking for several more minutes.

Finally, his mouth was empty of the honey.

"At first, I did not know if you were, like Sir William and Katherine, a Druid," Lord Baldwin began after clearing his throat. "After all, how easy to pretend anger at the two friends of which you made mention, cleverly concealing their names as if you did not know I was a Merlin. Anything to gain my confidence. But we have passed Jericho, and now I know you deserve my trust."

"Jericho?"

"My logic is thus. Sir William is a Druid. Were you a Merlin, it would not be to his advantage to tell you of the Crusader safe house there known to the knights of this land, nor to your advantage to tell you that *I* am a Merlin. Were you a Druid, he would have told you of the existence of the safe house—and instructed you to meet him there to discuss more plans to continue the deception you and he would have plotted against me. When you first told me that you might seek Jerusalem after a journey to St. Jean d'Acre, I wondered if you really meant to meet Sir William in Jericho—the one town where all travelers to Jerusalem rest."

Lord Baldwin licked his lips of the honey that stuck. "In Jericho, you did not seek the safe house, so I can happily conclude you are not an ally of Sir William. You truly are a Merlin. I can welcome you as my son. I shall earn your trust by sharing with you the great wealth of a long-lost secret. Then, we can return to England, and with what you know, we will defeat the Druids there."

Silence as they both pondered those words. Not even the groaning of the donkey reached them at their secluded resting place.

"The honey was sweet, was it not?" Thomas finally asked softly.

"You are generous not to take some yourself. And you have my thanks for the sweetness I enjoyed."

"Yes, very sweet. As sweet as the lies you may have told," Thomas continued in the same soft tones. He held up his hand to forestall Lord Baldwin. "I am not the fool you think me to be."

Lord Baldwin winced. But not from Thomas' words. He clutched his stomach, and his wince became a moan.

"If the honey does not settle well," Thomas said, "it is merely because of the time I spent at the market this morning in search of the poison it contains, the same poison that pains my donkey below."

Less than an hour later, Thomas was walking through the streets of Jericho. The anger on his face was not visible, nor the jutting of his jaw, for his face was well hidden in the shadows of the draping cloth that protected his head from the sun. Yet his determination was obvious, and many were those on the crowded streets who gave way before his marching strides.

Thomas did not hesitate as he approached his destination, a small inn tucked among the poorer dwellings of the city.

He brushed aside the protests of an old man at the door of the inn, and as he climbed the stone stairs that led to the second floor of the square building, he placed his hand on the hilt of the sword.

When he reached the door that he sought, he did not knock. Instead, he pushed hard with his shoulder, and popped the door inward.

As he entered past the still-swinging door, he pulled the sword loose and slashed air.

There was no one to challenge him. All four occupants of the room were lying on mats, well-bound, gagged, powerless, and unable to react to his sudden appearance.

Thomas stepped ahead, then turned so that he could face the half-open door. He kept his sword ready in his right hand, and with his left hand, pulled the bands of cloth from his head to reveal his face.

Only then, did one of the occupants react with a widening of her eyes.

"Yes, Katherine," Thomas said. There was no warmth in his voice. "Thomas. Perhaps you remember me?"

Her eyes remained wide.

Thomas glanced at the others. "Sir William," he said, with the same lack of warmth. "You prefer assassins as companions? Or do you miss my company?"

The knight only blinked. The other two men, Umar and Hadad, shook their heads no.

"You have my sympathy," Thomas said to them, with no sympathy at all. "For you two shall remain here."

With that, Thomas stepped forward and with a small knife, cut free the gags from Sir William's mouth.

"One may return," Sir William warned him. "The one who guards us."

"Then he shall taste steel," Thomas said. "A fight will serve as a useful outlet for my anger. You and she and all the others have mocked me with deception for too long. Except now I intend to find the truth."

Sir William merely repeated his warning. "Watch your back," he said.

Thomas ignored Umar and Hadad as he moved to cut Katherine's gag.

"Thomas . . ." she began, only to stop at the cold rage in his eyes.

"I will free you both," Thomas said. "Under one condition."

He loosed a leather water bag from his belt. "The condition that you drink from this."

"Water?" Katherine asked.

"Perhaps," Thomas said. "Why ask with such suspicion? If I meant you harm, I would kill you now instead of burdening myself with your presence as we travel."

Sir William spit remnant threads of the gag from his mouth. "Drink it, Katherine. If he insists upon such childish games, we must play. And quickly. For if our jailer returns. . . ."

"I will drink," Katherine said calmly.

Thomas squatted to offer her the mouth of the water bag. He held Katherine's head to steady it as he poured.

This soft hair. Those deep blue eyes. And the lips which drink.

He frowned at his weakness for those thoughts. Katherine took his frown for renewed anger.

"It is not what you think," she said.

"That remains to be discovered," Thomas said. He moved to Sir William to let him too drink.

Then Thomas stood. He drank heavily from the water bag, then tied the mouth shut, and hung it again from his belt.

"At the very least," observed Sir William, "let the other two men drink."

Thomas wiped his lips and shook his head.

"They have done you no harm, nor mean you any harm," Sir William insisted.

Thomas shook his head again, then leaned over with the knife to begin sawing at the rope which held Katherine's ankles together.

"It will not be a favor to let them drink," Thomas said. He grunted in effort as the hemp of the rope snapped apart. "For the water we shared contains a slow-acting poison."

2 2

Past Jericho, somewhere high in the mountainous hills—Thomas did not know how far from Jerusalem—they stopped at dusk. Because the hills were so steep, there were few villages and no towns. Had Thomas even wanted to risk another night at an inn, it would not have been possible. The choices were to travel during the night, or else set camp—and travel at night through these dark hills would be suicide.

Thomas began to build a fire as the other travelers unburdened the donkeys and unrolled blankets. When they finished, they stood near the fire, and all watched Thomas in sullen silence.

"You see, perhaps, that I brought much food," Thomas said cheerfully. "And that our donkeys carry bundles of kindling. You may expect then, many more nights like this."

No reply came. Nor did he expect one. For all three travelers had moved during the day in complete silence.

Thomas stood, placed his hands on his hips, and regarded them where they stood.

They stared back. Lord Baldwin on one side, still pale with illness. Katherine and Sir William on the other, almost pressed together in mutual distrust of their other traveling companions.

"Come, let us eat," Thomas said in the same cheerful tones. "Then we shall talk of many things."

"Eat?" Lord Baldwin grunted. "Not your food. For what potion will you surprise me with next?"

"Come, come," Thomas said. "No trust?"

Thomas grinned at Katherine and Sir William. If it bothered him that they did not smile back in return, he did not show it. "And you two," Thomas said, grin still wide, "you'll not trust my food either?"

They merely stared at him.

Thomas rubbed his hands together briskly, as might a man content to be with favored guests. "Well then," Thomas said. "Let me propose this. You three cook. And I'll eat my share of the food. That way you can be assured I'll not poison you again."

Silence.

So Thomas continued, "Besides, as I'll gladly explain after our meal, the poison already within you is sufficient for your deaths."

The flames had died to the red glow of embers, low enough so that Thomas could see beyond the fire to the shadows cast among the boulders by the moonlight, low enough so that the piercing white of the stars reached his eyes as he sat cross-legged at the edge of the fire.

"Hear ye, hear ye, all those gathered here today," Thomas said a low, mocking voice.

"Spare us the games," Lord Baldwin said.

Thomas raised his eyebrows, not caring that the effect would be lost in the darkness. "Such a foul disposition. Does your stomach ail you already?"

"We shared the same food," Lord Baldwin said. "Ask questions of your own stomach."

"Tsk, tsk," Thomas countered. "Must I remind you that it is not tonight's meal which should concern you, but rather the honey you ate earlier."

Thomas grinned to remember the shock on Lord Baldwin's face as he had unbound him in the presence of Sir William and Katherine. The man had been as helpless as a baby sheep during his convulsions after the poisoned honey, and had been easy to bind and leave in the shade of the rocks until Thomas' return with the two others.

"If it is not these actions for which I will despise you," Katherine said to break a silence that had lasted since leaving Jericho, "then it will be for the taunting manner in which you treat us."

"Your feelings concern me little," Thomas said, now deadly serious. "And if you prefer rage to mockery, you shall have your wish. You and Sir William travel with assassins who tried to take my life. Lord Baldwin tells me he is my father, yet keeps from me his acquaintance of the two of you. Whom shall I trust? And why should your deceptions *not* fill me with anger?"

Thomas continued to speak, his voice now quiet and cold. "Merlins and Druids. Druids and Merlins. For too long now I have been subjected to the whims of either side. For too long now, I have been uncertain of the identity of the people who so mysteriously appear and disappear in my life. That changed, however, in Jericho, and for that I owe much thanks to Lord Baldwin."

Lord Baldwin croaked from his side of the fire.

"Surprise? Or twinges of convulsions?"

The croak became a groan.

Thomas stood quickly, moved to the donkey and returned with a wineskin.

"Drink," he ordered Lord Baldwin. "Three large gulps. No more. No less."

The man hesitated.

"Don't be a fool," Thomas said. "If I wished you dead, I would have killed you earlier."

Lord Baldwin did as directed. Thomas took back the wineskin.

"Good," Thomas said. "Your stomach shall settle shortly."

Thomas patted the wineskin. "I expect Sir William and Katherine will be in need of this as well."

"You are vile," Katherine said tonelessly.

"The pot calls the kettle black," Thomas replied, with equal lack of heat. "And I have a story to tell."

2 3

Thomas settled again at the fire, and then gestured at Lord Baldwin. "This man had spent every night of our travels in sound sleep. Until Jericho. Then, while he assumed I slept, he crept out. I followed. Much to my surprise, he reached an inn at the center of the town. I dared not remain too close, and it wasn't until he left your room that I was able to slip over myself and peer through the keyhole. Much to my surprise, I discovered he had visited a certain knight and woman who had once held my trust."

Thomas paused. "There was something unnatural in the manner of which those in the room were asleep. As if they had fallen suddenly. So I entered the room and discovered that they had been cast into a spell of sleep, I assumed by potion, easily concocted with Merlin—or Druid—knowledge."

Katherine sat up, a movement that caught Thomas' eye.

He smiled inside. *Perhaps she did remember the kiss he had failed to resist as he had gazed at the perfect curves of her face that night in the candlelight. Perhaps he hadn't imagined her eyes open-*

ing for a startled moment during that kiss.

Thomas did not let that memory interrupt his story. "I could only conclude one thing. Whichever side each claimed—and you have both claimed to be Merlins—one was Druid. For why else would Lord Baldwin do such a thing unless he opposed you? My question, then became simple. Who is Druid? Who is Merlin?"

Katherine groaned and clutched her stomach.

Wordlessly, Thomas stood again, and offered her the wineskin. "Three gulps," he repeated. "No more. No less."

She accepted the wineskin quickly. Thomas waited until she finished then took the wineskin.

Before he sat, he offered the wineskin to Sir William. The offer was declined, and Thomas sat to resume the one-sided conversation.

"Who among us is Merlin?" he repeated. "A simple question which presented me a difficult problem. For lies are too simple, and I have been deceived again and again."

He tapped his chin, as if thinking through the problem for the first time. "It took many hours, but armed with the knowledge of my own training, I found a solution."

"Poison," Sir William said. His voice strained.

Thomas brought him the wineskin as confirmation and waited while Sir William drank.

"Yes," Thomas said when the knight finished. "Poison. There are many known to the Merlins and Druids. Some brutally fast. Some slow. And, as you well know, there are many potions to counter these poisons."

Thomas smiled. "This one poison has proven to be the perfect answer. The convulsions strike once or twice a day and will worsen as death approaches. Unless the countering potion is taken."

Thomas stopped and drank from the wineskin. "As Katherine and Sir William know, I too shared that same poison. For two reasons. You need not suspect the countering potion if I too drink it. And you will realize how important this countering potion is to your survival. For if we all need it, we will all stay together. One side—" Thomas pointed at Lord Baldwin, then shifted his finger to point at Sir William and Katherine"—must guard me from the other. For if I die, so do *all* of you."

"How so," Katherine challenged. "With you dead, we can merely share the potion."

"And when it runs out?" Thomas asked. "How will you replace it? For the dozens of combinations of poison, there are dozens of countering potions. You will not live long enough as you seek the ingredients."

Thomas held the wineskin high. "No, you will all guard me against the others. And you will all stay with me, for I shall continue to supply you with life."

Lord Baldwin snorted. "Thomas, my son, to what purpose must we remain with these two traitors?"

Thomas' face softened. "Would that I could believe you were my father." Yet his heart urged him in the opposite direction. *If he is my father and a Merlin, then Katherine is a Druid. Can I bear that pain much longer?*

Thomas gathered new thoughts. "From Lord Baldwin's pouch I have taken the letter from the old man," he said. "It speaks of a great treasure. Together, we shall find it. In so doing, it is ensured that the true Merlins possess it."

"How will you know which of us is Merlin?" Katherine asked softly. "For I will tell you now that Lord Baldwin is the traitor, but you have no reason to believe."

"Believe me," Thomas promised. "I shall know. And the final convulsions of death from the poison shall be punishment enough for the traitorous."

2 4

They approached Jerusalem shortly after dawn. For two hours they had moved along the road in the pale light that preceded the rise of the sun above the hills behind them.

When the sun finally rose high enough to begin to cast long shadows in front of them, Thomas began to feel an inexplicable mixture of joy and dread. For these mountains and hills too were as strangely familiar as the house of his boyhood in St. Jean d'Acre.

As the clouds began to break in the growing heat of the sun, Thomas found himself living the dream which had haunted him night after night since it had first appeared during his sleep on the Plains of Jezreel.

The hills—as in his dream—were shrouded in gray mist.

The donkeys plodded ahead, but Thomas was scarcely aware, so riveted was he upon the view in front. And he wondered if indeed he were asleep and this a dream . . . *the mist swirled, then cleared and rays of sunshine broke through from behind him, sunshine that lit an entire city across the valley, so that the beams of light danced golden and silver on the curved towers tall above whitened square houses that spread in all directions along the plateau of the mountain.*

He rubbed his eyes, and when he opened them, the city walls were still there, the beams of light still dancing golden and silver on the curved towers tall above whitened square houses that spread in all directions along the plateau of the mountain.

Thomas half expected, as in his dreams, that from the walls might come a dark figure, small with distance. It was early in the day, however, and no other travelers shared the road that wound down into the valley ahead of them and then up the other side to the city fortress that was Jerusalem.

Thomas did feel a peace to behold the Holy City, an almost mystical wave of joy and love that sometimes filled him during prayer, a peace at the realization of the presence of One so great He had created the world.

With this peace came the fear of the dream. All Thomas need do, even in the brightness of the early morning sun, was close his eyes to see the figure and its gray face, and with that vision to feel again the trembling panic.

"Thomas, my son," he heard the figure call in his mind. Almost against his will he closed his eyes and trusted the donkey to take him forward. *The wrinkles of the dark cloth folded around the figure. But still, the face was featureless and gray.*

"Thomas, my son," the stranger called again. *"Are you a Merlin?"*

Thomas jerked his eyes open, straining to whisper the word, "Father," and was suddenly grateful that he was in the lead, that neither Lord Baldwin nor the others could see his discomfort.

Thomas tried to forget the end of the dream, because he was awake and the donkeys were already beginning to descend into the valley at Jerusalem's feet. But the ending of his dream was there, and he could not lose it.

The figure who claimed to be his father transformed into a dragon; yet before Thomas could scream, the dragon became Sir William, swirling out of sudden mists with a sword upraised.

Thomas grabbed the tender skin on the inside of his arm and pinched as hard as he could. Anything to distract his thoughts.

Behind him rode Lord Baldwin and Sir William and Katherine. Ahead, the Holy City. And, if he was wrong in his desperate plan, his death awaited.

The donkeys plodded forward.

2 5

"**It has been** no easy task," Thomas said, "to find scholars with knowledge of a Jewish rebellion which occurred a thousand years ago. Not when I am forced to slink from street to street with my face hidden lest my light skin reveal my identity among the Mamelukes."

As Thomas shifted the weight of a small sack from one hand to the other, he did not tell his listeners of the wonder he felt to walk the same narrow streets that a thousand years earlier held a procession of people who followed and ridiculed a lone man before his death upon a cross on the hills of Calvary nearby. Thomas did not tell his listeners of the noises and smells and sights of this fascinating city that made it a pleasure to roam in his search.

His listeners were in no mood to appreciate any descriptions, something reinforced by Lord Baldwin's next words.

"Two days in this cramped hovel as we wait for you to return with food. Two days of wondering whether Mameluke soldiers will burst through the doors. Two days of watching the traitors opposite me to ensure that all of us live. I have little patience for *your* difficulties. Especially because I ache to help you, to prove to you I should be trusted."

Sir William sighed with weariness. "Lord Baldwin, it is no different for us."

Thomas surveyed the room. All three did look exhausted. Dark rings under Katherine's eyes showed the strain on her. *Yet fatigue does not diminish the beauty that shines from within.*

Thomas closed his eyes against the thought. *I cannot believe in her,* he told himself. *I cannot let my own heart betray me.*

"How long must this game continue?" Katherine asked. "It is to the point that I almost wish death would take me away from the nightly convulsions brought upon me by the poison."

Thomas shifted the sack again to the other hand.

"Did you not hear me?" Thomas asked. "I said it *has* been no easy task. Now it is completed. I have secured a map and—" he held up his sack "—provisions from the market which will let us begin the last part of our journey."

Thomas began to step past them into the other room. "Please begin to prepare for that journey. In a short time, I shall be ready, and I wish to leave with no delay."

He did not wait for their reply, but stepped through the curtain which served as a door.

In the other room—one smaller but just as poor and bare as the first—Thomas moved to the uneven wooden table in the center.

He removed the provisions from the sack and set them upon the table. There were several dried roots, a handful of dried seeds, a vial of dark liquid, and a small clay bottle with a fine, white powder.

Was there a movement at the doorway?

Thomas glanced up quickly, but saw nothing. He began to

shred the roots with a small knife, then froze at a startled scream cut short in the other room.

Before he could move, the curtain parted, and Sir William stepped through.

"You have no permission to enter," Thomas thundered.

Sir William stepped aside as Katherine half stumbled through the curtain.

"Nor you—"

Thomas stopped as he noticed the reason for Katherine's clumsy movement. A knife was held against her throat. And Lord Baldwin was pushing her forward.

"Do you wish her dead?" Lord Baldwin asked softly from behind her. His wolfish smile—which had been hidden for so many days—glinted again in triumph.

"No," Thomas said without hesitation.

"Then set upon the table your parchment map to the caves."

Thomas reached into his clothing and pulled out a small roll of parchment. He placed it on the table beside the roots.

"You had impressed me," Lord Baldwin said in conversational tones. His voice hardened immediately. "William, if you make another movement, this knife slashes her throat."

Sir William froze.

"Excellent," said Lord Baldwin. "Now stand beside Thomas. That way I can see you both."

Sir William joined Thomas at the table.

Lord Baldwin kept his left arm wrapped around Katherine. His right hand, which held the knife sharp against her throat, was steady.

He resumed his conversation.

"Yes, Thomas, you had impressed me greatly. Until your stupidity now. What else would you bring back from the market but more of the necessities of a countering potion?

Especially if we are about to embark on our journey again."

Thomas bowed his head. "Please forgive me, Sir William. I had not expected this. It would have only taken a moment to prepare this, but now. . . ."

Lord Baldwin laughed. "But now I will know the ingredients. I have no reason to remain among you."

Lord Baldwin tightened his grasp on Katherine and nicked her throat. Two drops of blood trickled downward.

"Finish your task, Thomas," Lord Baldwin snarled. "Do not delay."

Within minutes, Thomas had completed the mixing of ingredients.

"Pour it back into the wineskin."

Thomas did so.

"Excellent." Lord Baldwin thought for several seconds. "My choice would be that you die by the sword. My sword. But once I release Katherine, I cannot be sure of the results of battle. Not against two."

He thought for several more seconds. "Thomas, take the leather strips with which you bound me on the road from Jericho, and tie William's hands behind his back. I will test the bonds when you finish. If they are loose, Katherine dies."

The task lasted several minutes.

"Now, Thomas," Lord Baldwin said, "take the remaining leather strips, place them in your hands behind your back, and walk backward until you reach Katherine. She will bind your hands. At the slightest threat of movement from you, her throat will be cut."

The new task took slightly longer, for Katherine could not move quickly with the knife exerting pressure against her neck. When she had finished, Lord Baldwin reached forward and slid Thomas' sword from his sheath.

"Again, excellent," Lord Baldwin said. He pushed Thomas

forward with a rude kick. "Securely bound, I can kill you at my leisure."

"No," Katherine said.

"No?" Lord Baldwin asked. He released Katherine and stepped back, sword at the ready. "You make demands on me?"

"An offer," Katherine replied. "Their lives for my assistance."

Lord Baldwin snorted. "Your assistance? You are Merlin. I am Druid."

"As you travel," Katherine said, "it will be valuable to have a companion. I hardly dare kill you, not when you have the countering potion."

Lord Baldwin examined her and smiled. "A travel companion. I like it." He stopped stroking his chin. "And if I refuse your offer and kill them, but take you anyway?"

"I will fight you to my death," Katherine promised.

Lord Baldwin began to stroke his chin again.

"We shall bind their feet too. Then I will accept," he said, "but only because it gives me greater pleasure to think of these two facing a slower death from poison. For who is there to release them once you and I depart?"

2 6

Well, my friend, Sir William said in the silence that followed the departure of Lord Baldwin and Katherine, "death is not a pleasant prospect at any time. Yet I shall seek consolation in knowing you and I share the same fight."

Thomas sighed. "The actions of Lord Baldwin prove that we do share the same fight. I am baffled, however. The assassins of St. Jean d'Acre. They traveled with you to Nazareth. . . ."

"Please forgive me," Sir William said. He explained to Thomas the reasons for their actions.

"And Lord Baldwin is not my father," Thomas said, almost as a question.

"No."

"Then who?"

"I was sworn not to tell."

Thomas groaned.

"But now that we face death, he may understand if I break that oath."

A frown crossed Thomas' face.

Sir William noticed the frown. "How long before we die?"

The frown transformed into a brief smile. "Ask that question of God. Only He can foretell the day of a man's passing."

Sir William did not return the smile. "A poor jest, Thomas. God did not make me drink poison."

"Nor did I," Thomas replied. "And it is difficult to resist the temptation to threaten you with death to learn my father's name."

"Merely *threaten* me with death? But the poison we drank! The nightly convulsions!"

Thomas tested the bonds on his wrists and feet and winced at the bite of leather against skin.

"You may recall the predicament I faced in Jericho. Were you and Katherine Merlins? Or was it Lord Baldwin? One side claimed to be my father, yet met with you in secret. The other side—you—had threatened me with assassins, yet had been pursued in England by Druids. I knew I had to find a way for the Druid to be revealed."

"Yes, yes," Sir William said between grunts as he too tested his bonds.

"I devised a test, knowing that any Druid would gladly abandon a Merlin to die. As you can see, my logic has proven to be correct. For Lord Baldwin took the first opportunity given him. It was not stupidity—as he so quickly assumed— that led me to announce I had returned from the market. Rather, it was bait. Bait, I might add, upon which he pounced."

Sir William shook his head. "He could easily have killed us."

"I was desperate," Thomas replied. "And had he raised the sword, I would have announced that he still needed us alive."

"My head spins, Thomas. What could he need from us? He has the old man's letter. He has the parchment maps to the caves. He has the countering potion."

Thomas smiled. "Do you forget? There was no poison. Each evening meal you ingested a small amount of the juice squeezed from an insane root. Only enough to upset your stomach for ten minutes. The convulsions would have stopped whether or not you received the potion, which of course, was no countering potion but merely sweetened wine and water."

"You ate the same food we did," Sir William countered. "And *we* prepared it."

Thomas winked at the knight. "Who was it to deliver the *plates* for each meal? Plates—except for mine—smeared with tiny drops of poison."

The knight laughed. "Well done!" Then Sir William caught his breath. "But you said we held something of importance that would have stayed Lord Baldwin's sword from our throats."

"The map to the caves," Thomas said. "Knowing I wanted the Druid to take my bait, do you think I would also give him the map?"

Another laugh from Sir William. "The parchment he took is useless?"

Thomas nodded. He waited until Sir William finished laughing.

"There is more," Thomas said.

Sir William echoed his words. "More?"

"Yes. I expect we will be free within minutes."

"Impossible. I have given thought to our release and know it will be difficult, for I will have to use my teeth on the knots of your bonds."

"That too was my original intention. But since Katherine

departed with Lord Baldwin, our task will be much less difficult."

"Less?" Sir William strained against his bonds. "I am forced to disagree. Once we free ourselves, we must begin immediate pursuit to rescue Katherine."

Thomas began to whistle the tune of a childhood rhyme.

"What is it?" Sir William demanded. "What other knowledge have you kept from me?"

Thomas continued to whistle.

"Thomas!"

"My father's identity?"

"I have sworn the secret."

Thomas resumed whistling.

"If my hands were free . . ." Sir William threatened.

"If they were free?" a new voice came through the doorway.

"Katherine!" Sir William blurted.

She stepped through the curtain of the doorway. She smiled at Sir William, but only for a moment, for her gaze turned almost immediately to Thomas.

He stared back, hardly daring to let his face show the joy that consumed him.

Without breaking her gaze, she stepped forward and leaned over, as if to cut the bonds on Thomas' wrists with the small knife in her right hand.

But she did not use the knife. Instead, she kissed him. Lightly at first as she stood leaning over him. Then she fell to her knees, dropped the knife, and held his face in both hands and kissed him again, longer this time.

How long?

Thomas did not know. For his eyes were closed and his mind was filled with her touch and scent and the feeling of her hands on his face.

Discrete coughing finally reached his ears.

Sir William coughed louder.

Katherine released him but only drew her face back several inches.

"Thank you, Thomas," she whispered. She kissed him lightly again on the tip of his nose. "Thank you, my love."

Thomas could only grin like a dancing fool.

When he found his voice, he asked, "Where did Lord Baldwin fall?"

"Thomas!" Sir William's voice was a begging groan. "What has transpired?"

Katherine picked up the knife and still on her knees, began to saw at the bonds around Thomas' wrist.

"I can explain," she said. "Lord Baldwin drank the countering potion as we began to find our donkeys. Before he could offer it to me, he fell backward, holding his stomach in agony."

Thomas nodded. "My final weapon, Sir William. I brought back from the market—not the ingredients for a countering potion—but a vile poison."

"Your test could hardly have worked more perfectly," Sir William said.

Before Thomas could modestly agree, Katherine interrupted.

"Not so, Sir William," she said. "For when Lord Baldwin fell to the poison, he rolled in such agony that he drew the attention of many passersby."

Thomas and Sir William frowned.

"Among those passersby were Mameluke soldiers," Katherine continued. "They now search the city for all of us."

THE WINDS OF LIGHT CONTINUES ...

After a year of exile in the deserts of the Holy Land, Thomas of Magnus has discovered the final secrets of Magnus—only to learn a centuries-old battle depends on his next decisions.

In *Merlin's Destiny*, the temptations to abandon his faith are great, the promised rewards staggering beyond a man's dreams. To resist means the almost certain death of the woman who pledged him love forever.

And even if he finds a way to reach escape across the seas to England and Magnus, it may be far too late to win the final battle which has unfolded since the time of Merlin and King Arthur.

HISTORICAL NOTES

Readers may find it of interest that in the times in which the "Winds of Light" series is set, children were considered adults much earlier than now. By church law, for example, a bride had to be at least 12, a bridegroom 14. (This suggests that on occasion, marriage occurred at an even earlier age!)

It is not so unusual, then, to think of Thomas of Magnus becoming accepted as a leader by the age of 16; many would already consider him a man simply because of his age. Moreover, other "men" also became leaders at remarkably young ages during those times. King Richard II, for example, was only 14 years old when he rode out to face the leaders of the Peasant's Revolt in 1381.

Chapter One

The Crusades were a series of religious wars from the years A.D. 1095. (The First Crusade) to 1270 (The Eighth Crusade). These wars were organized by European powers to recover from Muslims (infidels) the Christian holy places in Palestine, especially the Holy City: Jerusalem.

Gradually, toward the end of the 1200s, the Muslims re-conquered all the cities which had been taken from them. St. Jean d'Acre, the common destination for all ships bearing Crusaders, was the last to fall to the Muslims, and remained in Christian hands until the year A.D. 1291.

Chapter Four

Though some scholars disagree, it is commonly held that Sun Tzu—a Chinese general and military genius who lived hundreds of years before Christ was born—compiled a book of his military theories and philosophies. This book has survived relatively unchanged for over 2,000 years; today, readers may find all of Sun Tzu's surviving military advice in a book titled *The Art of War*. Indeed, the quote used by Thomas from "the words of a wise general now long dead" is taken directly from that book.

Chapter Eight

A warrior race of Muslim Egypt, **Mamelukes** were originally non-Arab slaves to Egyptian rulers. They overthrew their rulers in the middle of the 1200s. Not only did they prove to be too powerful for the Crusaders, they were the only people ever to defeat a Mongol invasion—in the year A.D. 1260.

Chapter Fifteen

The earliest known records of **Druids** come from the 3rd century B.C., and according to the Roman general Julius Caesar (who is the principle source of today's information on Druids), this group of men studied ancient verse, natural philosophy, astronomy, and the lore of the gods. The principle doctrine of the Druids was that souls passed at death from one person to another.

Druids offered human victims for those who were in danger of death in battle or who were gravely ill. They sacrificed these victims by burning them in huge wickerwork images.

As mentioned in the letter of chapter eighteen, the Druids were suppressed in ancient Britain by the Roman conquerors in the first century A.D. If indeed the cult survived, it must have had to remain as secret as it was during Thomas' time.

Chapter Sixteen
Probably because of an excellent education, Sir William is acutely accurate in his observation of the **Dark Ages**, the term commonly given to the years A.D. 500–1000. These were centuries of decline across Europe, mostly attributed to the fall of the Roman Empire which left a vacuum of power that encouraged civil wars and stifled classical culture. This lack of education among the common people and the suspicion between countries prevented the sharing of ideas, especially in the arts, science, navigation, and medicine. (Interestingly enough, what culture there was remained preserved in remnants by monks of Ireland, Italy, France, and Britain.) Not until the **Renaissance** – A.D. 1350–A.D. 1650 – did modern civilization begin to flourish as men across Europe began again to strive to learn and share ideas.

Chapter Eighteen
Paper-making was invented in China in 100 B.C., another Chinese invention that remained unknown to the Europeans for hundreds of years. (See historical notes on gunpowder in *Wings of An Angel*, Volume 1 of "Winds of Light" series.) The Arabs learned how to make paper by questioning Chinese prisoners of war in A.D. 768. From there, it spread through the Arab Empire, which at that time included Spain. From Spain, paper-making finally spread to the rest of Europe.

Historical record shows that the **Second Jewish Revolt** took place in A.D. 132 and lasted for three and a half years. **Cassius Dio,** a Roman historian as noted in the letter, wrote a brief notice of the war which has survived to this day. In this notice, Dio relates that toward the end of the rebellion, Roman legionnaires were unable to engage the Jews in open battle because of the rough terrain, and instead were forced to hunt them down in small groups in the caves in which they hid and starve them out. Cassius Dio describes the final results this way: "Fifty of their [Jews] most important outposts and nine hundred and eighty-five of their most famous villages were razed to the ground. Five hundred and eighty thousand men were slain in the various raids and battles, and the number of those who perished from famine, disease, and fire was past finding out."

As also noted in the letter, the Roman general **Julius Severus** *was* summoned from Britain to end the rebellion. And a number of the mentioned **Dead Sea caves** were discovered in 1951-52 and 1960-61.

Chapter Twenty-Six

Insane root was widely known from Egypt to India. It is also known as fetid nightshade, poison tobacco, stinking nightshade, or black henbane. This plant contains the poisons hyoscyamine and atropine. Its seed and juice are deadly poison—even in small portions, it can cause death in fifteen minutes. Among the many symptoms are uncontrollable convulsions. It is probable that Thomas used extremely small doses of the poison to produce the results immediately after meals. It would have given two advantages: difficult to taste, and a slight tremor of convulsions which needed no countering potion to end naturally minutes later.